A Rose on Ninth Street

By

Joseph F. Ruggiero

ISBN: 0-7596-8107-4

This book is printed on acid free paper.

1stBooks - rev. 01/21/02

Acknowledgement

To all my family and friends who made this book possible and most especially my wife, the love of my life.

Special thanks to my daughter Jacqueline Jacobson and to my friend John Scioli.

Chapter One

It was eight o'clock in the morning and already the thermometers in the doorway of Pontello's produce store read eighty-eight. The trolley passed by slowly, clanging at the unruly boys to get out of the way. They ran helter skelter down the streets of the Italian Market. This area of South Philadelphia in the fifties could have been Italy. The huddled masses yearning to breathe free had duplicated their village markets. The tempo, the language, foods, smells, the deals and bargaining, it was undeniably little Italy.

Dominic and Maria Pontello were busy unpacking and carefully arranging the fruits and vegetables to make an attractive display for their outside bins. These stalls were the lure. They attracted the customers and once under the awnings, salesmanship made the bread and butter for these seasoned entrepreneurs.

Unpacking, sorting, piling, they bent over and straightened up like Sicilian peasants in the fields. After three generations the family had not escaped the backbreaking physical labor of farming in Sicily. The wages were better in America, but the hard work was the same. Maria heard what sounded like wheezing from her husband.

"Dominic, business is good, why don't you get yourself an assistant, a younger man, someone who can help you with the lifting and the carrying?"

"Why, you think I'm getting too old for the work?"

"Yes, you're getting older and wiser too. You don't have to prove anything to anyone no more. Stop doing it all by yourself. You don't have to anymore."

Dominic was stubborn. Still in good shape for a man in his sixties, but now he was making more noises than he did when the work was nothing for him even just ten years ago.

Maria and her older sister Theresa waited on the customers. Monica, the fourth generation Pontello, she worked everywhere,

1

inside, outside, in the back and on the street and doing the books. She was sent to business school for two years so that the family could dispense with the services of an accountant, a stranger, not even an Italian. This was the first year she did everything from bills of lading, ordering and quarterly taxes. The family had reached an even tighter level of functioning keeping as much as possible within the family.

Produce had a way of finding its way onto the street. To keep up the good appearance of this produce store and the wishes of the Ninth Street Merchants' Association, Monica and Aunt Theresa swept, hosed and cleaned the street as many as three times a day. Even though Monica was the new generation, she still grew up with the old ways of diligence, long hours of work and cleanliness.

Monica was inside helping her father with a crate of corn. Aunt Theresa was manning the stands with her broom and sharp eye for pigeons, flies and thieves. She was not afraid to use the broom on man or beast. Business was good. And she looked like a captain gazing self-satisfied upon his tidy ship and diligent crew. She stood with the broom at her side and her arms folded like the leader she was.

She wore her black leather apron on top of her black widow's dress. She was a type on the market, women widowed in their fifties who carried on the business like men. Those weren't bins of bananas, tomatoes, peppers, oranges and lemons she commanded. They were her life's blood, the blood of her dead husband and the blood of her relatives who made this business out of nothing but will and determination. It was no wonder that young Monica had special affection for her Aunt Theresa.

While the customers were milling about, a beggar came up to an elderly lady, who was picking through the peppers like a bird foraging for food. She was looking for crisp, thick and hollow sounding peppers. Like most of the customers she knew what she was looking for. The poor beggar did not choose

2

wisely. He snuck up behind the old lady and said, "Ma'am, could you spare some change for a poor man to get something to eat?"

She gave him a look of such disdain that he immediately turned to a man who was picking through bananas. "Sir, can you spare a poor man some change."

Aunt Theresa had a scowl on her face like a black rain cloud. She tightened the kerchief she always wore on her salt and pepper hair. She did this instinctively when she readied herself for war. But her preparations weren't enough to intimidate this beggar. "Why don't you leave my customers alone, you're a nuisance."

"Come on! Be a Christian, dear Lady!" The beggar hoped their shared religion would soften her heart.

"Christian I am, and a lady too but you're a lazy bum. Why don't you get a job and work like the rest of us."

The man holding the bananas said, "It's all right." He rifled through his pocket and dropped fifty cents into the beggar's hands.

"Thank you kindly, Sir. Thank you again, and God bless you. You see, some people know the meaning of Christianity."

"If you don't want my broom up your ass you'll get out of here right now. You should find yourself some honest work instead of sponging off others. I'll show you how a Christian works for a living."

The beggar slunk away but not before giving Theresa a gesture of disrespect. But now Aunt Theresa had to face a new challenge. Two guys were staring intently at her and they were standing dangerously close to the pears. One had a tattoo with a skeleton head embossed on his upper right arm, a sign of gang membership. The other had a very bad case of acne.

"What are you looking at, you pimple faced moron." Aunt Theresa didn't mince with the English.

"An old hag," said the pimple faced boy.

The boy with the tattoo said, "Would you like to dance?"

"Well too bad for you that this old hag has good eyes. I saw you thieving magpies stealing fruit from Bruno's stand

3

yesterday. Move on; move on before I call the cops! Then we'll dance. When they cart you away I'll dance a tarantella."

"Before I call the cops, before she calls the cops. The old hag's calling the cops. The old hag's calling the cops." The boys sang in chorus.

Theresa didn't call for help. She didn't work hard lifting and carrying without developing some upper arm strength. She wanted a shot at the big guy with the tattoo. Her left hook and the broom would do it.

Before she could lay him out, a young Irish boy came by. It seemed like he knew the two characters. He said something to the boys and they disappeared as quickly as they had appeared.

Monica came out and said, "What's the problem Aunt Theresa? Is this guy giving you a hard time?"

"No not him, but I think a couple of his friends were trying to see what I was made of. But when he came along, he told them something, and they just left. What'd you say to them two hoodlums?"

The boy said, "I just told them to leave hard working people alone, and go mind their own business or they would have to deal with me."

Monica said, "That was nice and courteous of you."

The Irish boy said, "Well, I had an ulterior motive, actually I am looking for a job."

Theresa said, "We don't need no help. When we need help we get it from the family. Thanks for getting rid of those two criminals. Take a pear and then you can leave too."

"Aunt Theresa, let me at least ask him his name."

"My name is Bob, what's yours?"

"My name is Monica. And this here is my Aunt Theresa.

Pleased to meet you Bob, but I have to go inside now."

Monica went inside the store. The counter was piled high with paper work. No time to talk not even to good-looking young boys, especially since she was already spoken for.

Bob had no intention of leaving. He was smitten. He followed Monica into the store like a man trying to sell a car or

4

more like a puppy dog following his master. He didn't take his eyes off her. She was a little over five feet tall, with olive skin and she wore a plain blue dress with a black leather apron on top. He could tell she had sway when she walked, and that struck him as very feminine. He already caught sight of her round, plump breasts and her elegant and shapely legs. She was an attractive young woman but probably spoken for he thought, the way these Italians marry so young in their late teens. But that wouldn't stop him. This boy had confidence and a mission.

He said, "If you don't mind, I would like to properly introduce myself. My name is Robert O'Connor and I want to work here in this store doing anything that needs being done."

She turned to him surprised that he followed her into the store and not a little pleased. "Like my Aunt said, we only hire family." She couldn't take her eyes off his tattoo. It was a cross and under the cross was etched in caps MOM.

He said, "Are you looking at my tattoo?"

"Yes, I didn't mean to stare, I just found it interesting."

Actually it told her that this boy respected his mother, which was a good thing in the fifties. Girls liked when boys respected their moms. It was a promise of a good man, someone who might make a good mate. And she took in more than his tattoo. This young man was a looker with his white tee shirt and muscles, but not the brawny kind like a weight lifter's. He had the body of a runner or maybe a swimmer. Then she looked away ashamed of herself, looking at another man when she was already engaged.

As she was thinking all of this Mr. Dominic Pontello, her father, stepped into the room from the back, "Can I help you young man, are you being waited on?"

"Daddy, he isn't a customer. He wants a job, but I already told him we are a family business and that we only hire family."

"But sir, my mother is sick and I need to make money to help her out. There's a first time for everything. I can work as hard as family. The reason I want to work is for my family."

"Where are you from, sonny?"

"Eighth and Mifflin, Sir. Look, I really need work. Like I said my Mom is really sick and I have to help out. I'll work hard, I promise. Just try me out for a day."

"Wait here a couple minutes. I want to discuss this with the family. Maria and Monica, could I talk to you?" They excused themselves and went into the back room.

The boy walked nervously around the store. He was agitated. If he didn't get a job he didn't know what he would do. He might have to steal or do something desperate. But his mother needed to be taken care of. He wanted to help his mom the right way, but would he get the chance to do it through honest work? He couldn't stand watching her deteriorate but he would do whatever had to be done to help her. His father wasn't reliable. Someone had to take his place, even if it meant breaking the law. But there was nothing that would give him more pleasure than working legitimately, especially anywhere near this girl Monica. What a natural beauty! No make up; raven black hair, and a voice that could melt lead. He knew girls before but not like this one. He wondered if he had a chance. If confidence were all it would take, the girl was his, but she looked like she was strong and would not go for just anybody. Anyway these Italians stuck pretty much to themselves. Irish wasn't an easy in.

Monica came out of the back room with her parents. She wore a smile ear to ear. Her mother spoke, "You look like you might be a hard worker. We'll give you a chance. But you're gonna have to do a lot of lifting since Mr. Pontello is having some back trouble. So if you're willing to work like family, we'll take a chance on you."

"Son, you got to be here three a.m. everyday, Monday through Saturday. We have to pick up the fruits and vegetables at the terminal. And you have to load and unload the truck. Then we work a full day at the store. I'll pay you a dollar above minimum wage and we'll talk in a couple months about more permanent arrangements."

"Mrs. Pontello, Mr. Pontello, thank you for giving me a chance. You won't regret hiring me. You'll see."

Aunt Theresa came in from outside. "Theresa, I hired an assistant for Dominic. He's a wise man to get help at his age. Maybe we can keep him around a lot longer."

"Si vuole Di'! If God wills! Welcome to the family business. Let me get you an apron and some work. We'll test those muscles of yours. And if you sleep on the job you'll get my foot up your ass, and you'll be out on the street where you came from, you blue eyed Irish devil. You stay away from my niece. I saw how you were looking at her. You seen my broom, but I'm pretty good with my fists if you want to try me."

Monica said, "Aunt Theresa, remember he's gonna work like family. Don't worry about who does what looking. I'm not a child anymore. Anyway I think he's a gentleman. So give him a chance."

Aunt Theresa led Bob away for orientation, Italian style. She said, as she held the broom in the air like a number one, "He gets one chance."

The Irish boy laughed and followed his new manager. His prayers were answered. Help would come to his mother the right way. He was getting too old and grown up for the gang.

Just as Theresa was about to orient her new employee, Dominic said, "Theresa, offer the boy some lentil soup. It's on the stove in the back. Since he's gonna work until nine tonight, we better feed him."

Monica said, "You see Bob, you're like family already. They want to feed you." She cut short her smile when she saw Pasqual walking toward the store, all six feet of him limping from when he fell off a trolley when he was twelve.

He took one look at Bob standing next to his Monica and asked him, "Who are you?"

Dominic said, "I just hired him. His name is Bob. He's from the neighborhood."

"I thought you only hired family?"

"You know, Maria convinced me that I needed help especially with the heavy stuff. This boy is built for work." In the meantime Bob had extended his hand to Pasqual.

7

He said, "Hello, my name is Robert. Pleased to meet you. Are you a relative?"

"I am Monica's fiancé." Then Pasqual turned to Monica and said, "Can I take you down the street for a quick lunch?"

"I'd love to go, but I'm up to my ears in book work."

"That's okay, I'll be seeing you tonight anyway." He gave her a peck on the cheek and Monica turned beet red. Before he left he looked over his shoulder and said to Bob, "These Pontellos are good people. I'm practically a member of the family. It would be very upsetting if someone took advantage of them, if you know what I mean."

Bob said, "Well I guess we can't let that happen now can we?" Pasqual bit his lower lip and gave Bob a long unfriendly stare and crossed the street.

Aunt Theresa said, "Well I don't know about anyone else but I'm eating lunch al fresco. Anyone care to join me?"

Monica suggested, "Aunt Theresa, I'll get you your soup and lemonade. Bob and I will eat in the kitchen. The fan is on in the kitchen and I want to get out of the heat." Monica didn't know why, but she felt strangely alive today, almost giddy. For some reason she liked Bob and had a good feeling about him being in her family, as a laborer, of course.

And she wondered if perhaps Pasqual hadn't been a little unfriendly to him. Never mind Pasqual, she'd see him tonight. He'll get over this new person on the scene. She was not one to over process things or worry needlessly. She brought burly Aunt Theresa her midday meal. Soup in hand, bread resting on a pile of pears and the broom temporarily leaning in the doorway, the guardian of the produce ate with great satisfaction.

Meanwhile, Monica and Bob sat at the table by the stove and chatted like old friends. The fan was blowing Monica's hair in its draft.

Bob said, "You know Monica, outside the sun really brightened your brown eyes and olive skin. And with this fan going, you look like a movie star walking on the beach.

She said, "The sun does that to us Italian girls. And you flatter me, comparing me to a movie star. I don't suppose you ever were close to an Italian girl?"

"Can't say that I have. Not that I wouldn't like it."

She wanted to change the subject. "What kind of work you been doing?"

"Odd jobs and things, you know, mostly laborer kinds of jobs. I had to leave high school to help out at home. Did you finish high school?"

"Oh my yes, mom and dad sent me to business school for two years. I have an associate's degree in bookkeeping. I love this business, and now that I can do the books I feel like they really need me. You know the mayor even comes to this store. Someday I hope to be able to manage it for my mom and dad when they get too old to work."

"Gee, I wish I could have finished but, there are some problems with my dad. I'll tell you sometime. But even without finishing I have been able to help out my family, but it's harder when you work with your body instead of your mind. What's with Pasqual?"

"We are engaged, you know?"

"I don't picture the two of you together. Do you love him?"

"We are engaged!"

"I'm so sorry. I meant no offense, it's just that…"

Dominic came into the room, "I think you better hurry the lunch along. I got a shipment of grapes coming in and I want to unload them carefully."

"Yes sir, I am ready and have eaten my soup, and just one more bite of this delicious bread and I am yours completely."

"That's the spirit, Bob. He'll do fine, don't you think, Monica?"

They left Monica alone with her thoughts, a place she would rather not have been. Something wasn't right. She didn't tell Bob that she loved Pasqual. The question might have been fresh, but why hadn't she declared publicly her love for Pasqual Greco, her fiancé? She was sorry her dad came into the room. She would have liked to get to know Bob a little better.

Who was this Bob O'Connor? What was there about him that so attracted her? She never remembered feeling this way about any boy in her life, even Pasqual. It was something more than his good looks and politeness. There was a drive in him, a resoluteness that was very manly and very attractive. He was a family man and would fight for his mother and struggle as best as he could to put food on the table.

She guessed that his father was probably in the rackets or maybe an alcoholic. No matter, Bob was good. A virgin that she was, there were stirrings in her that she was not aware of. Nor would she be, considering her strict upbringing. If she could have named them, she would have said that he had awakened in her, feelings of deep sexual attraction.

Chapter Two

When Bob left work, he found John and Leo playing cards on his front steps.

John said, "What kept you so long? We been killing time for two hours already."

Bob said, "Who asked you to wait? Why didn't you go get a job like I did today instead of harassing old women? When are you going to grow up? It's like you're still ringing doorbells and running away."

"Oh, Bob's gone legit. Now we all got to fall in line and become respectable like him," said Leo. "What are you wasting your time with minimum wage when you can make a hundred times more on the streets?"

"I'm tired of the streets. I'm tired of running away from the cops. Besides there are other things in life."

John said, "Like sweethearts? You got a crush on that Italian girl."

Bob answered, "You leave her out of this unless you want my fist down your throat. They're nice people and they are off limits or you'll have to answer to me."

Leo said, "Bob, you don't have to talk tough to us. Remember we're your friends, we knew you when. We just got to get used to the new you."

"I'm sorry. I didn't mean to come off like the tough guy, it's just that I got to pick up my mother at the hospital. She's going through tests. She will be undergoing serious surgery in a few days. My grandmother and I got to pick her up tonight."

John said, "We understand. We all got it rough in some way or other. We'll leave your new friends alone. You go with your grandmother and take your mother home where she belongs. And remember you don't make no money working for nobody else but yourself. So when you come up short, remember we're friends. When you make new friends don't go throwing out the old, understand?"

11

"Yeah, I understand. Look I gotta go."

He left his friends in a confused state. This was Bob, a leader, and maybe second in command of the gang. Was he going soft on them, all of a sudden, in one day because of some girl he met for a couple of hours? No, as soon as his mother got better he'd be back in there swinging for his gang.

Chapter Three

Bob met his grandmother on the second floor Oncology Care Unit. She looked younger than his mother did. She was healthy; seventy with blue eyes and ivory skin. If only his mother could have looked that good at fifty. The oncology nurse greeted Bob and his grandmother, "Well, Mrs. McDermott, I see you have someone with you today."

"Yes, my grandson, Bob."

"Well, it's good he came because we have another half hour of testing before we can release Mrs. O'Connor and you can keep one another company." She directed them to the waiting room across the hall from the nurse's station.

Bob was struck by the patients who were all ages, little boys with no hair, older men with lesions on their thin-skinned foreheads, some people minus limbs. It was the distressing look of cancer, the biggest taker of human life in the fifties. Bob saw a young man who was about his own age. He was wasted away like a concentration camp victim. *Is this how it ends?* Cycled and recycled through his brain.

This was the first time he was convinced that there was no hope for his mother. He saw through the pseudo-science, the desperate medicine that kept the medical scam alive at the expense of his mother's hopes. Maybe his mother knew the truth already. He knew he couldn't let go, even in the face of this despair. He couldn't think of life without her. He had hoped to make her happy one day to make up for his father's abuse, to show her a good time, give her grandkids, a nice home and some laughs before she died. She couldn't die now the way things were.

For half an hour the television played Milton Berle. It was painful ignoring the comedy. He would have rather waited in a quiet place alone with his thoughts. The oncology nurse came over to them and told them, "It's time to see Mrs. O'Connor. You're going to have to let her rest for fifteen minutes before she'll have the strength to go home. In the meantime I want to explain to Bob the treatment and what to expect." Mrs. McDermott went in to see her daughter.

Bob had a question, before she got started, "Will treatment cure my mother? All these people seem so sick. Treatment didn't seem to help them."

"We hope, but there is no guarantee. Your mother is seriously ill, but you must not give up hope. She will have the best of treatment that is available today."

"The doctor told me that my mom got breast cancer in an advanced stage. Why don't you tell me the truth, her days are numbered."

"Bob, I wouldn't be so negative, like I said, there is always hope that they can get at the cancer."

"What kind of treatment will they give her?"

"An operation. It's called a radical mastectomy, removing the breast."

"You can't do that," said Bob, jumping up from his chair. The nurse calmed him down and said, "You must understand. If you want your mother to have any chance of surviving, she must have this surgery. It will not only take her breasts, but the cancer with it. We then must keep a close watch on her and hope the cancer never returns."

"But your not even telling me...What are her chances to survive?"

"Bob, that's a question only God can answer. We do our best. Now go see your mother and bring her some good cheer. Get rid of those glum looks. She needs to be encouraged. That's a part of healing that you can do. Go in there and lift her spirits. I won't let you in unless you cheer up. Got it?"

Despite himself Bob smiled, "Got it and thank you, Ma'am."

"That's the spirit."

Bob was surprised to see his mother seated in a chair. She looked at Bob and smiled. "It's you, Bob. Can we go home now, I'm tired of this place." Grandmom left to bring the car around the front of the hospital. "I'll meet you out front in a few minutes. Bob; make sure your mother sits down at the entrance. I don't want to find her standing waiting for me to come."

As soon as grandmom left Bob's mom said, "You know, she's getting a little forgetful. Just before you came in she said 'I have to help you clean your house.' And she already cleaned yesterday."

"She can clean everyday of the week, she's that strong, but how do you feel?"

"I feel fine, just a little weak. The doctor said I'll be fine."

He looked at his mom and thought, another doctor lying to make a patient feel good. The cancer had already made her complexion wan and tired looking. He wondered what other humiliations lay ahead. They met grandmom in front of the hospital, and in five minutes they were home. Grandmom had already prepared meat loaf, roasted potatoes and corn. Bob's mom just picked at her food. Grandmom said, "Eat up, eat, it's good for you."

"Mom, it looks great, just don't have much of an appetite."

"Force yourself!"

"Mom, put a platter aside for Jim. He probably hasn't eaten all day."

Bob thought there she goes worrying about that drunken worthless bum. He said, "I don't know why you worry so much about him. He can take care of himself and anyway he doesn't care about anyone but himself."

Margaret O'Connor said, "Bob, don't speak that way about your father. Whether you like it or not, he is still your father and you owe him respect."

After dinner Bob announced that he was going to bed. "Going to bed, it's not even ten o'clock."

"Mom, I got a job today at Pontello's Produce. I have to be at work at three a.m."

"Bob, that's great. This could be the start of a new life for you. I'm so happy."

Bob went upstairs to bed, smiling to himself. He got his mother to smile. He was doing the right thing, and already it helped his mom a little bit.

Sleep wouldn't come, as much as Bob wanted to sleep. He lay there in the dark ruminating about his father, how his mom would send him out to look for him, how he disappeared sometimes for days at a time. He thought how much he hated going into saloons, embarrassed, knowing that his father was the object of ridicule. All he could think of was big fat Murphy, wiping down the tables and the thirty foot long bar. "Son, you dad's in the back. You better take him home. He won't make it on his own." Then the scene played itself out again in painstaking detail. There was the sound of barking coming through the open door of the back room. "Now bark, Fido, bark and I'll give you some whiskey."

Fido barked on command. But it wasn't a dog. The eight year old Bob went back and saw his father on all fours with his head down and a big overgrown three hundred pound man named Bill was holding a bottle of whiskey and a shot glass. He filled the shot glass to the brim. Again the command, "Bark, Fido, bark! Be a good doggie and bark and I'll give you whiskey."

Jim looked up and saw his little boy. "Son, you shouldn't be here." This was the first time he heard his father address him so gently as son, and in this awful place, and him barking like a dog to get another drink.

"Mom sent me to get you. She's worried sick and wants you home."

"Go home, son. Tell your mother I'll be home in a little bit."

"It's been two days, Dad. Come on let's go." The guy holding the bottle, Bill said, "Why don't you listen to your father? Go home like a good boy!"

"No, leave him alone. All you want to do is make fun of him."

"I ain't making no fool of nobody. We're just good friends having a little fun. Now I said get out of here, before I get nasty."

"Why don't you leave my dad alone? You're not his friend. You're only making a fool of him." Bob turned to the group and repeated himself. A few of the men answered in chorus, "Get out of here, kid. Go home."

Bill grabbed hold of Bob's arm, "Go home, Bob!"

"Leave me alone, you big ape."

"You little piece of shit, show your elders some respect or I'll kick your ass." Bob's dad came front and center and slurred, "Leave him alone, Bill."

Bill turned around and knocked Jim on his backside with one good shove, "Stay out of this you rummy!"

Bob cried, "Leave my father alone," and with that he kicked his ankle. Bill became furious and slapped Bob and before anyone could do anything about it, Jim was standing behind Bill with a chair suspended over his head. He hit the back of Bill's head and forced him to the ground. Everyone was shocked because Jimmy was a passive drunk. Bob was amazed. He never thought his father would have the courage to stick up for him.

Bill was on the floor, "You're going to pay for this, you son of a bitch. You will have to be carried out of this room."

Big fat Murphy barreled into the room. "Enough of this, you guys. The party's over. You've had your fun, and we got a child in the room. Jim isn't your mascot, and he's going home with his little boy. Bill, you had it coming to you the way you string Jimmy out all the time. Bill, you keep your hands off Jim. I'll settle any scores that need settling. Now, Jimmy, go home with your boy. Your wife is waiting for you."

Then all Bob could think about was how his mother washed him up, treated him with love and compassion, fed him and put him to bed like he was her baby. Bob loved his dad, but he had mixed feelings now that his mother was sick. He thought his dad should be doing more for her who had done so much for him. It was hard hating your father while the eight-year-old boy inside of him loved him unconditionally. Like a mantra Bob found sleep repeating to himself, I don't want to hate him, he's my dad, I don't want to hate him, he's my father, I love him. The scene had exhausted him once again. Bob was too old to cry himself to sleep, that all stopped when he grew up.

Chapter Four

A month had passed since the Pontello's hired Bob O'Connor. It didn't take long for Bob to show his worth. Bob and Dominic had just returned from the waterfront produce supply houses. Dominic said, "Hey Bob, how about a cold drink before we unload the truck?"

Bob said, "No thanks Mr. Pontello, I'd rather unload the truck first."

"Bob, I'm already impressed with your dedication, but I don't want you to overdue it in this heat."

"I'm fine, Mr.Pontello. Anyway work helps me forget my troubles."

"A young man like you with his whole life in front of him, what troubles could you have?" Before Bob could answer, Maria called for Dominic.

"Coming, Maria!"

Bob finished unloading the truck and was about to enter the store when Monica appeared in the doorway. She looked radiant in her yellow sleeveless dress. He didn't know what to say. He wanted to say that she was just about the most beautiful girl he had ever met and would she go out with him, and forget about that creep Pasqual, with his refined airs, manicured nails and money. Greco's meat market! He wouldn't love Monica the way a girl like her deserved. All he could manage was a clumsy predictable greeting, "Hello, Monica, another hot day!"

"Bob, the heat doesn't seem to bother you any. I wish you could have heard all the nice things my parents are saying about you in the store."

"That's good to hear. But it's like I told your dad, hard work helps me clear my head and forget about my problems."

"I know, it's your mom again."

"Yeah, well what can I do. Seen your boyfriend lately?"

"Yes, he's just fine, thank you."

"I haven't seen him around the store lately."

"Well, you know, he manages his father's store."

"Yeah, Greco's Meat Market. I guess you see him in the evening?"

"Well, we are engaged. We see one another quite often."

"If you don't think your boyfriend would mind, could I maybe take you out for a donut and a cup of coffee?"

"I don't think he'd mind. We do trust one another and a cup of coffee is hardly a date."

Bob smiled despite himself. He knew it was a date and he had made his first inroad on his competitor's territory. "See you after work, Monica."

Monica's face turned red. "See you, now don't go killing yourself. They already think the sun rises and sets on you. You have nothing to prove. Okay, till later." She went into the store with her invoices and numbers and he stayed outside with Aunt Theresa, dressing and watering the fruits and vegetables, making small talk with the customers and generally passing the day with busy but light work. He kept watching the clock for quitting time. He couldn't wait to be alone with Monica.

It was a welcome break when Theresa called for more bananas and strawberries. He got a chance to go inside and pass by Monica, who just looked up from her work and gave him a warm smile. Bob was let out early to go home and clean up in order to take his mother to the hospital.

He went into the store, "Monica, can you go with me now for some coffee? I'm through for the day and I got to take my mother to the hospital for more testing."

"If you're running late we can make it some other time."

"No, of course I have enough time. Come on let's go. You need a break just like I do. Those numbers must buzz around your head after a while."

When Monica and Bob came out of the store together, old hawk eyes, Aunt Theresa noticed them side by side. "And where are we going at three thirty?"

"Aunt Theresa, Bob suggested I go with him for a cup of coffee." Aunt Theresa gave one of her dark scowls. "Monica, you know how jealous Pasqual is. Why are you tempting yourself?"

Bob answered, "Aunt Theresa, what harm is there in a cup of coffee? I could use the company, what with going to the hospital with my mother."

Aunt Theresa said, "You want company, I'm available." They both laughed. And she said, "I'm no fool. I know what is going on. There's an old Italian saying he talks about the saddle but means the horse. You two just better be careful. The next time I'm coming with you. Now get out of here before I beat Bob senseless with my broom. Pasqual better not come by looking for you."

"Oh, Aunt Theresa, we're engaged."

"Exactly! Now go, and you, young lady, you be back here in half an hour or I'll come looking for you. Bob, I hope your mom is feeling better. I started a Novena to the Little Flower that she get better."

Bob couldn't even say thank you; he was touched by this seemingly hard woman's offer of prayers. If he had said a word he would have dissolved in a flood of tears. He and Monica walked side by side like discreet lovers, which they weren't yet, but they walked comfortably with one another to Joe's Donuts and Coffee Shop.

Monica broke the silence. "I hope you know that we all like the work you are doing for us and are glad you asked for a job. I'm just sad that your mom is always on your mind. I wish I could help you."

"Thank you, Monica, but just sitting here with you, having a cup of coffee is all the help I need. Monica, I really like you, I mean, not in a dating way, but I really like being with you and I feel less burdened in your company and you have always been so friendly to me."

"Bob, I feel the same way about you. Can I ask you a personal question?"

"Anything Monica!"

"Does your father help out at all?"

"Monica, my dad's just about the biggest disappointment in my whole life. He was never there when you needed him and he stays away for days at a time and my mother still worries about him and can't do enough for him when he shows up. He should be doing for her. I don't know why she puts up with it all."

She cupped his hands in hers and said, "Bob, she loves him. Don't you understand what that means? She loves him, they were probably childhood sweethearts, and she feels very deeply for him. Don't be mad at him. He can't help himself. And to tell you the truth, when you fall in love, sometimes there is no choosing. It just happens and you're in it for better or for worse."

Her touch was electrifying, both consoling and arousing, giving him the courage to bring up her fiancé again, "Is that how you love Pasqual?"

"Always Pasqual! What do you want me to say, I'm engaged."

"I want you to tell me you love him more than any other person you have ever met and that he is the man for you."

"Don't you think you're out of line getting personal like that?" It was too late for Bob to mount an excuse or explanation, because Pasqual was standing beside them at the table. "Hello, Monica!"

"Oh, Pasqual, hello, sit down and have a cup of coffee with Bob and me. I was keeping Bob some company before he went to take his mother to the hospital."

"Well now isn't this cozy. You're consoling poor Bob because his mother's in the hospital."

"That sounds mean Pasqual. No one has done anything wrong here," said Monica.

Bob was nowhere near as conciliatory. "If you don't like what you think is going on here, we can take it outside like men."

"That's just the way I see it, you low life Irish punk."

"Pasqual, Bob!"

"This guy is scum. Why are you letting yourself be seen with him in public? Everyone knows that we are engaged."

"I'm not a piece of meat that two dogs are fighting over. I am engaged, and you have to have a little trust. If either one of you lays a finger on the other I'll have nothing, absolutely nothing to do with either one of you. When you come over my house tonight, Pasqual, you better put this thing way behind you or we're through, and I mean it."

She stormed out of the shop; Pasqual followed like a whipped pup. Neither he nor Bob dared say another word to one another. They knew she meant it.

Bob was alone with his coffee. He looked over to where Monica had just been sitting, where they had been communicating so beautifully and a pain seared through his heart.

Would he ever win this girl over to what he was sure was love? He had two problems, his dying mother and this love, which had not yet come to life. He paid the bill, left a generous tip and flew out of the shop to his home where his mother was waiting for him.

In the meantime Pasqual had caught up with Monica. "Monica, I'm sorry. I didn't want to make a scene and embarrass you in public."

"Then why'd you do it? I was so mortified. Joe knows mom and dad. Probably everyone on the market knows what just happened. You know how people like to talk."

"Well, what do you expect. I see you with this other guy and we are engaged…"

Interrupting him, "And you got jealous, and you don't trust me, and you want to put a leash around my neck and control my goings and comings. It won't work like that with me. You don't own me. You have to trust me and put a loving interpretation on anything you see me doing. I did nothing wrong. That is what love is all about, trust. No, leave me alone. I'll get over this, but I just want you to leave me alone."

They had reached Pontello's Produce. Monica broke away from Pasqual and into the store without turning back. Aunt Theresa took it all in and just glanced at Pasqual and knew the whole story. She said to Pasqual, "You know son, sometimes we have to take the long way around to get what we want. Monica is headstrong. The tighter you hold onto her the more you will lose your grip. Control your jealousy! Trust Monica or you might lose to the Irish boy. That ethnic stuff is wearing thin. We're in America now. The old ways have to give way to the new. Listen to an old lady!"

"Thank you, Aunt Theresa, I'll try." He walked away and Aunt Theresa, sweeping clean with her new broom, just shook her head. She thought, *he's* too *set in his ways to change. The poor bastard is too Italian for his own good.*

Chapter Five

The trolleys rode more smoothly this morning. The streets weren't crowded with customers, just merchants preparing to open for business as usual. Dominic and Bob were busy unloading produce and Monica was reconciling receipts from the previous day. The first chance she got, she was going to apologize for her part in the scene at the coffee shop. The harsh words said in the middle of Bob's conversation about his mother, she just didn't think it was right and felt somehow to blame. Theresa and Maria were outside readying the stalls for the morning rush of customers. Theresa spotted the beggar.

"Look what 's coming this way. Where's the broom? I am going to shove this thing up his ass as far as his throat. He won't be able to beg for a month." The beggar was wearing an addled baseball cap, badly worn shoes and no socks. His gray hair curled from his unshaven cheeks and the upper part of his nose had caked on blood. His left eye was swollen. Aunt Theresa spoke first, "So, Mister Bum, looks like you got into a fight. Begging somewhere that you didn't belong? If you don't leave immediately I'll blacken your other eye."

The beggar said, "I'm here on business."

"What business you got here. We ain't no soup kitchen."

"I'm here to see my son."

Maria said, "What son? You got a son here? You're not related to Bob, are you?"

The beggar said, "That's who I came to see. Like I said, I came to see my son. And you ain't going to stop me."

When Bob saw his dad standing there, he had a look of terror on his face. He and Dominic were both carrying a crate of fruit. Bob's load slipped to the ground as he saw his dad. He wanted to tell Monica himself that his dad was an alcoholic, not have her find out this way. If Pasqual hadn't come he would have revealed everything.

"What are you doing here, dad? This is where I work."

"I had to talk to you, Bob. It's really important."

"Mr. Pontello, would you excuse me for just a minute?"

"Of course, Bob, take all the time you need."

Bob took his father out of earshot of the Pontello's, into the street. You could tell by the sounds that Bob was hollering at his dad. Dominic said to his wife, "Did you smell that man's breath? It was enough to knock you over."

Maria said, "Such a nice boy, I can't believe that beggar is his dad. It's such a pity."

Pasqual came down the street from his father's store. He passed by Bob and the man he was speaking to without a word, still afraid of Monica's threat. He said, "What's going on?"

Maria spoke, "Bob is talking with his dad."

"His dad, I knew they were low lives." He called after Monica in the store. "Hey, Monica, come out here. I want you to see something."

Monica came to the stalls, "What's up, Pasqual? I came to apologize for yesterday in the coffee shop. But look in the street. That bum, that's Bob's dad. Now I hope you see why I was so upset. These people aren't like us. They are white trash."

Monica said, "That's a terrible thing to say about any human being. That's Bob's dad and because we respect Bob we have to respect his dad. What kind of a half-baked apology was that? You're sorry and Bob's white trash. You don't even know what made me angry. It's because you didn't *trust me.* Do you understand, *trust me.* I don't have to prove myself to you. I already told you I loved you a hundred times."

"Mr. And Mrs. Pontello can't you talk some sense into Monica. I do trust her. She doesn't understand my fears."

Dominic said, "Monica, you have to listen to Pasqual. He has your best interests at heart."

Maria said, "Monica, we all like Bob, but you can't socialize with the help."

Monica spoke to Pasqual first, "And just what are you afraid of, you, a grown man, with a lot of responsibility, engaged to me. What are you afraid of?"

"I'm afraid you are letting this low life charm you into liking him."

"You think I am some idiot who doesn't know her mind and needs advice from her mom and dad and you on who she can and cannot have a cup of coffee with."

Maria and Dominic said, "Monica, don't get upset, we just don't want to see you get hurt." Their words overlapped. Maria tried to put her arms on Monica's shoulder and Monica pulled away, angry and hurt.

"This whole conversation is ridiculous. Pasqual, maybe you should reconsider if you want to marry someone as foolish, naïve and gullible as you think I am. How could you ever trust such a simpleton." She stormed into the store and shut the two doors in anger and to give her some space to nurse her wounded feelings. But she couldn't take her eyes off the father and son drama taking place in the street in front of the store. Her heart went out to Bob. She knew he was humiliated and embarrassed and she knew that you don't choose your relatives. It was apparent Bob had given his father some money, and he was walking away. She had to admit with tears in her eyes that she indeed had strong feelings for this Bob, whom her parents mistrusted and her fiancé hated.

A police car pulled up to the store, just as it opened. Dominic met the police in the doorway. "Good day, officers, what can I do for you?"

"We're looking for a boy named Bob O'Connor. He is a suspect in a break in on Jeweler's row, which took place a little after five yesterday."

Bob was just crushing some boxes on the side and heard the entire conversation. "Officers, I am Bob O'Connor and I was at Joe's Donut and Coffee Shop, before going home to take my mother to the hospital."

"Well, you are a prime suspect. We'll have to place you under arrest and take you to the roundhouse. If anyone can substantiate your story, they should appear at the arraignment this afternoon." They read Bob his rights and cuffed him.

Monica came outside and said that she could vouch for Bob's alibi because she was with him. She even had another witness, Pasqual Greco who had seen them both. She would bring him along to the hearing. Aunt Theresa took all of this in, sweeping and eavesdropping at the same time. After all it did take place under the awnings, by the stalls, in front of the main entrance, her territory.

Bob was ushered to the back seat of the police car, his head gently lowered by the police, so that he didn't bump his head and they whisked him away. Dominic turned to his daughter with an I-told-you-so-look on his face. Monica beat him to the punch," I don't want to hear it, Daddy. This is America, a man is innocent until proven guilty, and I know this man is innocent because I was with him."

Maria said, "Dominic, remember your pressure, let her go. She's a very sensitive girl; she never gave us any trouble. Let's just give her some space to sort things out. Come on, this is going to be a busy day. Right Theresa?"

Theresa, leaning on her broom, said, "Right, Dominic! If you can't see that the girl is in love you're an old fool."

"You mean Pasqual?"

"Pasqual, my ass, your daughter's in love with the pretty boy, the Irish. If you don't want to lose your daughter, you better realize that she is following her heart. She's got a fatal disease, she's crazy in love with this American."

Maria started to cry, "What if he is a burglar?"

Theresa said, "There's only one rotten apple in that family and he just hit his son up for some money. He ain't no burglar. He's in love too, in case you didn't notice."

Dominic said, "Then I should do something. The Greco's have money and prestige. Pasqual will give my daughter a secure and respectable life."

Theresa had the last word, "Okay, Dominic, don't listen to me. Hold on to your illusions. Pasqual means as much to her as my broom. You might as well take my broom and sweep the sky as to fight the powerful forces attracting those two. The old ways

28

are gone, Dom. Money and prestige meant something to us. We're not in Sicily. Kids today marry for love, not with security on their minds, and I am not so sure that they are wrong."

They went to the hearing, everyone except Maria and Theresa. When Bob's case came before the magistrate both Pasqual and Monica accounted for Bob's whereabouts during the time of the crime. A call by the clerk to Hahneman Hospital confirmed Bob's presence there and the fact that his mother was indeed undergoing testing. Bob was informed that his wallet had been found at the crime scene in the store on Jeweler's Row. Bob registered for the record that the wallet had been missing for over a week and had no idea of how it could have ended up in a jewelry store. The police had their own ideas. They were certain it wasn't Bob, but wouldn't discount his friends.

When Bob was released Monica was so relieved, "Bob, I feel so bad that you had to go through this."

Pasqual said, "Look Monica, I did what I said I would, now let's go home."

Monica said, "I thought we'd go and have a cup of coffee to celebrate Bob's innocence."

Pasqual said, "Innocence, don't you know that his friends probably had something to do with this. No offense Monica, but I think Bob knows some unsavory people, people I don't want any fiancé of mine hanging around with. I don't even want you hanging around with Bob outside the store."

Dominic said, "Listen to Pasqual, Bob is a great employee but no socializing and that's an order."

Bob said, "Monica, I'm bad news. Between my charges and my dad showing up at work intoxicated, pan handling. They're right, I'm not good enough for you." Bob broke away, and left the building without another word.

Monica said, "Dad, you know I love and respect you, but no one can tell me something is bad when I know it to be good. And as far as you are concerned Pasqual, I am not your or anyone else's fiancé. Only my father can talk to me the way you just did. I want to marry a man I love and respect. I already have a good father. The man I marry has to trust me and respect me and know I have a level head on my shoulders, and never will I spend the rest of my life with someone who orders me around. We're not in Sicily anymore." She broke away from father and fiancé and ran after Bob.

All Monica knew was that Bob lived on Mifflin Street. She headed toward Mifflin Street, which was on the way to Joe's Donut and Coffee Shop. There she found Bob sitting on a bench outside the store, which had established his alibi. He was hunched over with his head in his hands, obviously distraught.

She took her place beside him. Despite his utter despair, her presence made him happy, but not to the level of a smile. "Monica, why did you follow me? I'm bad news. Why don't you forget that you ever knew me?"

"Do you really want me to forget you?"

"For your own good, yes!"

"Bob, I'm a big girl now."

"I already caused arguments between you and Pasqual."

"Why don't you let me worry about that?"

"Don't you understand," he said as he rose to his feet. "We come from different worlds. Irish and Italians don't mix. I belong, I mean I belonged to a gang. We fought Italian gangs, and they sometimes target Italian businesses for harassment."

"Bob, I don't see any gang here. Just you and me, and I care about what happens to you."

"And Monica, if you don't know I care about you, you just haven't been noticing."

"Bob I notice everything. You don't look at me like I am an Italian; you look at me, Monica. And when I see you I see Bob."

Bob was about to say I love you and he couldn't take the chance just yet for fear of losing Monica completely. "Monica, I got to go home. My mom was very sick last night, and my grandmother has been spending the entire day with her and I have to give her some relief."

"Go do what you should do, your mother needs you. I'll see you at work tomorrow. Promise me you'll show up."

"I can't promise."

"At least tell me you'll think about it!"

"Okay, I will." As Bob was leaving Monica asked for his street number.

"1620 Mifflin Street."

Chapter Six

When Bob and his grandmother returned home from the hospital with his mother, she couldn't make it up the front steps. She was stooped over and holding on to the railing. The doctor told his grandmother and Bob that Margaret Mary was failing fast. They would not be able to operate. She barely had the strength to make it up the stairs even with Bob and her mother on either side of her. Once inside the house they led her to her favorite easy chair in the parlor. She fell into the chair like a sack of potatoes and breathed a deep sigh of relief. Bob's father came down the stairs.

With all the strength and kindness she could muster she pleaded with her husband, "Jimmy, please don't go out. Stay with me. I need your company."

"Margaret Mary, I'll only be out for a little while. Mom and Bob are here with you. You'll be all right."

Almost desperate, Margaret tried again, "Jimmy, please, I want you with me now."

Bob said, "Can't you see Mom needs you. What do you have to do that's so important? Can't you put your needs aside for once?"

"Bob, don't fight with your father."

Jimmy said, "I don't have to stand around for this. Like I said, I'll be right back. And you, son, mind your manner."

"Manners, mind your drinking, you alcoholic bastard." It was too late. Jimmy was out the door and missed his son's angry censure.

"Bob, he's your father, he's all you got. You two have to learn how to get along. I was hoping I would live to see the day he went to AA and cleaned himself up. When he was young he treated me like his sweetheart. He really loves you and me. Promise me you'll get along."

"Okay, Mom, I promise. I'll do anything to make you happy."

"I know, you were a very good son. No mother could have hoped for more."

"What do you mean was? I still am a good son." Grandmom called from the kitchen. She was preparing a meal while her son-in-law took the easy way out.

"Bob, you go eat. Tell grandmom, all I want is a cup of tea and some toast. I don't have much of an appetite and I couldn't keep a full meal down. But you go eat. You need your strength. I love you Bob, more than I could ever express. I can only say I love you with all my heart. You made me the happiest woman in the world. I am so proud of you."

"Why are you talking that way mom, you ain't going nowhere. I'll be right back with your tea."

Margaret Mary watched her son go into the dining room and disappear into the kitchen. She looked at her sewing machine that had served her so well in life. She had used the dining room as her work area. They never entertained. The four chairs from Good Will were never used for anything but to hang a jacket, or a skirt she had been altering. The table may have had a fruit bowl in the center, but there was no fruit, just the addled look of a chipped wood veneer table.

She had so little, yet she was thankful for so many things, especially that she could keep her little family together with her talents as a seamstress. Up until three months ago she made good wages at Industrial Draperies. And over the years people in the neighborhood came to her for alterations. She was able to burn her mortgage five years ago. Fifteen years of hard work, one stitch at a time, hiding what she had accumulated as best she could from her husband.

A month ago she went to O'Reilly's Funeral Home and prepared her own funeral. Paid for the coffin, the ushers, the priest, everything. She still had a few thousand dollars in a secret bank account, which she would leave to Bob. Unfortunately the home would go to her husband and she feared the worst. Her breathing became more labored. She knew she was dying.

Bob came into the room cheerfully like the oncology nurse told him to be, to lift his mother's spirits. He was carrying a plastic tray, with a melmac cup and saucer, faded green with tea. On the side were two slices of toast on which grandmom had spread some strawberry marmalade.

"Mom it's not much, but grandmom said it was brewed with love. Mom, what's wrong?" He heard this heavy breathing, almost like the sound of someone drowning. When his mother didn't answer he called after his grandmom. "Nanna, come quick, hurry, something's wrong with mom!"

"I'll be right there, hold on," she yelled from the kitchen. By the time she arrived the wheezing sounds of drowning had turned to a gurgle, what they used to call the death rattle, and Margaret Mary was dead in her son's arms. "Mom, don't leave me. I need you." Grandmom put her own grief aside and sat down next to her grandson. "It's gonna be all right Bob." She put her face next to his and his warm tears blended with hers as she drew him closer with her other arm. "Bob, she was in great pain. Now she can't suffer anymore." Grandmom took Margaret Mary's lifeless hand into her own and said, "Oh dear Lord, it's not right that the old should bury the young." Addressing Bob, she said, "I guess the Lord will keep me here as long as you need me, Bob." Bob couldn't hear a thing. "Oh grandmom, why did she have to die? Why couldn't they help her? She was so good." And his tears poured out upon his dead mother's hands, a fit tribute to the earthen tools that kept her world together.

"Bob, we got to make some calls. We got to get a doctor here to pronounce her dead and give a death certificate, or they'll have to take her back to the hospital and chop her up for some stupid autopsy. And we got to get O'Reilly's over here to take care of her funeral. Come on Bob, we got to do that for your mother. Now! We can cry today, tomorrow and the rest of our lives, but now we got to do for her like she did for all of us her entire life."

The calls were made. An autopsy was unnecessary. The family doctor listed the cause of death as breast cancer.

Grandmom told O'Reilly's that she would pay for everything, but it would take her three months to get all the payments made. She went on and on about what bonds she could touch, how much she could withdraw, and what her monthly social security check would allow and, finally, he had to interrupt her, "Mrs. McDermott, your daughter made all of the arrangements last month. Everything is paid in full. The only thing you might want to do is have a few of your neighbors and friends prepare a meal for after the burial."

Bob had just left to get some folding chairs from the funeral parlor for the visitors who would drop by at the house before the wake. Grandmom just sat down in a chair and rocked back and forth. "My Margaret Mary, she knew all along. She had so much faith and courage. You know Mr. O'Reilly, what the Irish say about a person named Mary?" The undertaker, who had knelt down beside grandmom and was just rubbing her back, said, "Yes, Mrs. McDermott, every Mary has a cross to bear. Yes, I know."

Grandmom added, "And she bore hers with dignity and not a drop of self-pity."

The undertaker stayed until Bob returned with the chairs. His men had already removed the corpse. There was nothing left but to go through the ritual motions of the funeral, the predictable consoling steps of waking, mass, internment and the ritual post-burial meal, then the long silence when the grieving should begin in earnest.

Bob, despite himself and wanting to grieve over the loss of his mother, was exhausted. Arrested, exonerated, his mother dying in his arms, he went up to his room, as soon as he hit the bed he fell asleep immediately with his clothes on. His grandmother gently removed his shoes and covered him with an afghan. She went into the tiny back room that was never heated properly and lay awake on the studio couch. She lay there in the dark praying the rosary, stopping from time to time to blow her nose and wipe the tears from her eyes. She regretted that she

35

lived so long to see the day when she would bury her own daughter.

Around two-thirty a.m. just after the bars closed, she heard what must have been Jimmy coming home, probably in a drunken stupor. She quickly got up from the couch and went downstairs. Jimmy said, "Where's Margaret Mary?"

"She's over O'Reilly's."

"What's she doing there?"

"Jimmy, Margaret Mary is dead. She's dead and she's at the undertakers, and he is preparing her for her wake."

"She's not dead Where's Bob?"

"He's asleep and he is dead tired. Don't wake him up. She died in his arms about a half-hour after you left, and said that you'd be right back."

"Oh no, this can't be. I need Margaret Mary. She can't be dead."

"Jimmy, I've been a good mother-in-law. I've minded my own business. I treated you with respect, and I never interfered. But I'm gonna step over that line I've observed for over twenty years. Margaret Mary needed you and you couldn't put aside your drinking for one half-hour to be there when she died. She's dead, do you hear me, she's dead and you weren't there and she begged you to stay. Now you live with that. I won't. I was here, and so was Bob. I don't care if you never talk to me again, but you were wrong. And she still loved you. I'm not going to say another word because, Jimmy, *she really loved you.*"

From the depths of his soul he groaned, covered his face in shame and cried and sobbed and there was no one to console him. Grandmom went to bed, closed the door to the back room and Bob never heard his tears, pleas for forgiveness nor his regret. Jimmy was healing and didn't know it. Jimmy hit bottom. What his wife could never achieve in life, she accomplished with her death.

Chapter Seven

The evening of the wake was the first time Monica got an opportunity to see Mrs. O'Connor, Bob's mom. It actually was a viewing of the lifeless remains of a poor cancer victim emaciated by her sickness. But her features were soft and her face must have been beautiful, because even in death, she had the look of someone whose face looked strange with make-up. This was the wake of a very simple, loving woman, the salt of the earth that never lost its strength.

Even in death Bob was proud of his mother. It was as if he had wanted to introduce his mom to the girl he had spoken so much about. His father and he sat on opposite ends of a mohair couch, recessed a little from the coffin. There was the kneeler in front of the bier, and Monica paid her prayerful respects before acknowledging Bob's presence. The woman reminded her of her own mother, she thought and cried, aren't we women all the same: loving, faithful, and dutiful until death. Why did God make it that way? It seemed that women suffered more and that the death of a woman was mostly sad, but partly like being taken down from the cross.

Monica said, as she embraced her fellow employee, "Bob, I am sorry for your loss." Before Bob could recover from her show of affection, Aunt Theresa, without the broom, was paying her respects to the dead, followed by Maria and Dominic. Maria and Dominic said nothing, shook Bob's hand. Maria kissed him on the cheeks, and Dominic handed him an envelope of money. "You always need a little extra at times like this." Bob was overwhelmed at their appearance and barely had the presence of mind to say thank you. Bob reluctantly introduced his father who, to Bob's amazement, had been sober for the last three days. He could not believe Aunt Theresa's diplomacy. Here she was offering sympathy to a man, when just a little while ago, she wanted to shove a broom up his ass.

Monica was the last to leave. "We'll see you at the store." Bob could only shake his head, not in agreement or denial, he was just so overwhelmed by Monica's affection, her parents generosity, and Aunt Theresa's bear hug. He wasn't all too sure that he would return to his job, but this was not time for a discussion. He called after Monica, "Will I see you tomorrow?"

She said, "Of course, I'll be in church." If you could be happy at your mother's wake, Bob was ecstatic.

The rest of the evening was almost easy. Monica's presence with her entire family took much of the sting out of his mourning. Too bad his grandmother wasn't there to meet these good people. She was in bed under Doctors orders. Running back and forth to the hospital and the shock of her daughter's death weakened her. If she wanted to attend the funeral the next day, she was to do nothing but rest. Since the mass meant everything to her, she would gladly forgo the wake, which she thought a grizzly pagan practice, anyway.

Something else strange was happening. This was the first and longest time Jimmy O'Connor had been sober. He almost made sense and was extremely polite and grateful for all the sympathy shown him and his estranged son. Bob wanted to warm up to him, but years of habit held him back, but this too would give in time. His promise to his mother, his childhood memories all worked against his present alienation.

And if his father would join AA, the walls would come tumbling down. Bob was still afraid to hope. He never doubted he loved his dad but disappointment and despair always tempered that love. He saw good things happening, and he wouldn't let himself think the painful thought that death sometimes accomplishes the answers to asked and unasked prayers. He didn't want to think that his mother had to die for good to come to him and his dad, but that may well have been the sobering and painful truth about God's ways that are so strange to us creatures.

When the last visitors had left Jimmy turned to his son and said, "Bob, are you hungry, can I get you a steak sandwich or a hoagie? Pat's is still open."

"That sounds great. I haven't eaten anything all day. Yeah, that's a great idea. I want mine smothered in fried onions with sauce on the side and a quart of coke."

They went out, side by side, father and son for the first time in years.

Chapter Eight

When Bob and his father entered the church behind the coffin draped in black, Bob immediately saw Monica in the last pew. Despite the somber moment he smiled from ear to ear when their eyes met. He wanted to lock his eyes in place. Monica put her head down in humility and out of respect.

The procession of people was not long. It was a small family, but there were a good number of neighbors and friends. But still Monica would not leave her last place. Bob would have wanted her by his side, which would have been disrespectful to her. She would soon find out that he always wanted her by his side. Her presence kept eating into his grief. She gave him hope for a happier future. In his wishful thinking, he had them as man and wife. Monica's feelings were growing in that direction, only there was a great stumbling block. It wasn't Pasqual as much as it was her loyalty and character. She had accepted a ring. She was betrothed to another.

The priest was an old man. He had baptized Margaret Mary, gave her first communion, prepared her for confirmation and had officiated at her wedding. Now he was burying her. "Death is sad. Even Jesus mourned when his friend died, but death is also good. The person who dies we know is in a better place. They are beyond suffering, pain and disappointment. They see with the eyes of God. And their death is sometimes a jump-start for change for those of us who are left behind. But when a good person dies, there is rejoicing in heaven and on earth. Margaret Mary was a good person. She comforted the sick by making bandages for the missions and the Hawthorne Sisters cancer hospice in the city. She fed the hungry. She made casseroles for St. John's Hospice where the homeless go to eat. I delivered them for her myself. She sewed the altar clothes, ironed and starched them for twenty years. Her nimble fingers crocheted and sewed vestment for priests at our parish and for the missions. She worked hard everyday of her life and the last three months of her life, she worked at dying. Without self-pity she visited the rectory, paid me for the singer and organist. When I refused a stipend for her funeral mass, she wouldn't leave unless I took the money as an offering for masses for the poor souls in purgatory. Her only concerns were for her husband and her young son, just twenty years old. Her own death did not frighten her. Her confidence in God's loving providence gave her peace. She understood human limitations. She had no time to fret or worry. She would have liked to have seen a grandchild, but she believed that she would continue to care for and love her family in heaven. The last thing she said to me was, 'Father, I have known the love of a husband, the joy of giving birth to a loving son and the gift of loving parents. I am returning to God with gratitude and faith. If St. Theresa of the Little Flower, my patron saint, in her simplicity could say, I will spend my heaven doing good on earth, will God deny me just a little bit of that pleasure for my little family. No, he won't. I am going to a good Lord who knows my unfinished work. She hugged me and I gave her the Irish blessing. And I can only say this to you, Jim, Robert, Mrs. McDermott, family, friends and neighbors, we bury today a woman who, because she only knew how to love, could only expect the same from God. May we all live in such a way so that when death comes to us, we can go to God without fear, without hesitation, with full confidence that he will love us as we have loved others. Go and love one another, be like your heavenly Father, be like Margaret Mary. Do not pity Margaret Mary, imitate her and rejoice that God created such a person in our neighborhood, in our lifetime."

This sermon left Monica sad. She loved two men and, for never having met Mrs. O'Connor, she knew her. She was in love with her son and Monica herself had many of the same qualities that the priest alluded to in his words of comfort. Most boys, and most girls, marry people like their mother. It was clear Bob was headed in the right direction. Monica wondered how Mrs. O'Connor would solve her present dilemma, loving Pasqual and loving Bob. She had no confidence that there would be an easy solution nor did she think she had the ability to satisfy two men in search of her life long devotion, without bitterly disappointing the one or the other.

Monica resolved to speak with Bob at the house, after the burial and tell him things that might at first hurt but would bring her conscience peace and Bob, ultimately, understanding. Those were her intentions. She left the church feeling that somehow Mrs. O'Connor had heard her prayers and interceded for her. Monica too had that kind of faith.

Chapter Nine

In those middle years of the last century neighbors would often provide the meal after the burial. Since Mrs. O'Connor had cooked for others and had been a kind and considerate neighbor, the meal was lavish, even by our standards. Even as the family was returning home neighbors were still bringing in cherry, apple and early pumpkin pies. Pound cakes that needed no icing, they were so well made, were already on the table. The home smelled of freshly brewed coffee and on the kitchen stove were pots of meatballs, hot roast beef sliced thin and already in brown gravy, and veal and peppers. The table in the tiny dining room was filled with homemade potato salad, macaroni salad and cole slaw. One party hip neighbor had made celery sticks stuffed with cream cheese, deviled eggs, a crab salad dip with potato chips, Spanish olives and salad nicoise with fresh tuna her husband had caught in the Atlantic. Nothing was too good for Margaret Mary.

Monica began with an apology. "Bob, I am sorry my parents and Aunt Theresa couldn't make it to the Mass and burial. They hoped you would understand that we couldn't shut the store down on a business day. I hope I am enough of a representation that we care about you and are sorry for your loss."

"Of course, I understand." He reached over and kissed her quickly on the lips. "I'm just so glad you were here. I wish my mom could have met you." He picked up a plate and handed it to her.

"Oh Bob, I'm sorry, I can't stay. I've been away from the store over half the day."

"With all this food! You haven't eaten all day; you were at the Mass and the burial. Surely you are hungry."

"I'll get something on the run at the store. My dad wanted me to make sure I welcomed you back."

"I appreciate his offer. When can I see you again?"

"When you come back to work."

"Not sooner? What if I don't come back?"

"Well, I really hope that won't be the case."

"Monica, something's different."

"What do you mean, different?"

"You just seem a little distant. Did something happen?

"Nothing happened."

"You answered too quickly. You've been so thoughtful, been with me through this whole ordeal and now you want to pull away without a bite to eat."

"I told you my parents need me."

"And your parents didn't need you all day up until now? You're holding something back. What are you keeping from me?"

"Bob I didn't want to tell you all of this the day you buried your mother. And I care too much about you to come off like I'm holding something back. It's just that I have mixed feelings." Bob knew immediately what she was hinting at.

He said, "I'm listening."

"I'm engaged to Pasqual. He is a good man and I just can't forget him."

"Okay, he's a good man. You don't marry someone because they are good. There has to be love."

"Don't you understand, I do love him and… Bob I am very fond of you and my feelings for you are pulling me in the opposite direction, away from Pasqual."

"How long have you known him?"

"All my life, Bob."

"Well then you should know whether or not you love him and no one, not even me could pull you in any other direction."

"That's what I thought, Bob. Then the other night I was alone and thinking of the good times we had together. I thought of our wedding plans and then I realized there might not be a wedding. Suddenly I felt so empty and lonely. If I didn't love him why did I feel this way?"

"Maybe because you're afraid of something new?"

"Well, I'm not so sure it's that easy. Later on that evening Pasqual visited me. He poured his heart out to me. He said,

'Monica, I know I'm a proud man. I'm a jealous man. I know I don't have to tell you that. I am also stubborn, but I got to thinking all day today. I need you. I love you. I don't know what I would do if I lost you.' That was the first time he ever admitted that he needed me. He told me many times that he loved me but never that he needed me. He told me he would come back in a few days. He knows my feelings about you. He's not stupid. He wanted to give me time to think."

"Monica, I need you too."

"Bob, I got to go. I am so confused. You go back to your guests. We'll talk later." She turned and went out the front door. He stood in the doorway fixed on Monica as she walked down the street. He was sure he had lost her. He was very close to tears when his friend John was approaching his house from the opposite direction. "I see the boss's daughter paid her respects. You're still going after the new friends and forgetting your old."

"Thanks for coming, John."

"Bob, me and the other guys are real sorry. They'll all be stopping by later. You've been through a lot. You need a little fun, you've been brooding too long." John didn't know that he was brooding over two women. "I'll be over tomorrow night, you me and the boys will go out and let the good times roll."

"Good idea, John, now you come in and see what a feast my mom's friends have made to her honor. I can't brood forever. I haven't eaten all day and you, John, have given me an appetite."

Chapter Ten

Bob's Dad had been floating around all day, talking small talk, something he hadn't done for years in his dazed stupor. He still didn't realize the full extent of the losses he sustained in the death of his childhood sweetheart, Margaret Mary. He would in the days to come, however, realize the growth that was taking place inside of him because of that same loss. As far as Bob was concerned, he approached Bob almost in fear. He knew he deserved the boy's anger for not being there when his wife died.

It was true that Bob was angry, but it was softened by the pity he felt for his father, still that little boy inside of him who saw him humiliated by his so called friends at Murphy's was afraid to let himself be proud of his father's behavior since his mom died because of the countless disappointments in the past. Even though there wasn't much time left, Bob would grow to understand his father's love and eventually put to rest his anger, along with all the other foolishness of childhood. With grandmom acting as homemaker, there was light on the horizon. At the cemetery Bob and his dad shared a tearful embrace.

That night after the burial Bob, his dad and grandmom stayed home to comfort one another through simple quiet and the healing presence of one another joined by Margaret Mary's love. They did what most people do in like situations; they reminisced, pulled out photo albums and ate leftovers that would last them at least a week. The phone rang and grandmom answered. It was John. In a voice filled with apprehension and suspicion she said, "Bob, it's John, he says he's a friend of yours." Bob took the phone out of her limp hand and said, "Hey, John, what's up?"

"We still on for tomorrow night, remember, all grief and no play makes you dumb."

"You got it, man. I'm looking forward to being with all of you. Tomorrow night around eight, Okay!"

He wasn't off the phone a second, when grandmom stepped in and said, sounding a lot like Bob's mother, "I don't like your friends. They're trouble makers."

"Why do you say that?"

"All they do is hang on the corner and get drunk."

"So what, they're not bad guys."

"That's not what I hear."

"You can't believe everything you hear."

Then Jimmy came into the room with an announcement that stunned them both.

He said, "Mom, Bob, there's an AA meeting at the church at nine o'clock. I think I'll leave now so I won't be late." Grandmom and Bob looked at one another. She was already in tears. Bob had to fight hard to keep from crying. They just said goodbye like he was going to the store. "See you at breakfast dad, I'm going to turn in early. Everything has finally caught up to me."

Grandmom reminded Jimmy to lock up when he went to bed. She was going to try and sleep also. That night when Jimmy returned from the meeting the house was still, just like the night Margaret Mary died but in Jimmy's heart there was a fullness he could never put into words. Like a trickling of water that becomes a creek, that becomes a stream and then a river, something was growing in him that would never stop. Could this be grace and the answer to a lifetime of faithful prayer?

Chapter Eleven

John called again at noon. "Hey, Bob, we'll meet you at six. We're going to a carnival. Are you up to it?"

"I can't wait. See you at six." He called up the stairs to where granny was making the beds. "Granny, John called and I'm going to a carnival at six."

His friends were at the front door. Granny held him by the shirt sleeve. "Please, Bob, don't go, stay home tonight." He kissed her on the cheek, "It'll be fine. There's nothing to worry about. Just me and my friends going to a carnival."

It was a muggy late September day in Philadelphia. Indian summer with moist air. Leo and John had brought along the drinks. "Leo, pass the drinks around, offer Bob first."

"No, John, you know I don't like to drink. Too much sadness and pain."

John wouldn't be dissuaded, "Just a few swigs. How you gonna have any fun if you don't light up just a little? You been through a lot these last three days. Lighten up, come on!"

"Okay, just a swig." Bob tasted the cold beer and it ignited a passion in him that he hadn't felt in years. He would try and forget the pain of his mother's death and what he was certain was the loss of Monica. It was like the first night he drank with the guys when he was twelve. He downed half the bottle, wiped his lips with the back of his hand. "Now that's the spirit, Bob, now you're one of us again." John turned to the guys and smiled. That night John was the leader; he always called most of the shots. He was immature but thought because he was persuasive and could get the other guys to do criminal things, he must be the leader. Leo clung to him and was his flunky. He got his in by being the leader's go-get-it man. Two others were there, Nick the fat stutterer, and Jim who liked to fight. And there was also one gun. One gun and five fools.

When they saw the cops coming they jettisoned the beer down the sewer and moved with a purpose to the field opposite the stadium where the carnival was being held. On the way John told them the latest neighborhood gossip. "Did you hear about what happened between this white couple walking the fair grounds and this here black kid walks by and makes a pass at the white girl, right in front of her boyfriend. Then later when it gets dark, and this here nigger returns with two of his chronies and one of them attempts a rape, while they beat up the white guy. A couple of people from the crowd caught sight of what was happening and they broke it up before anything happened. If we see them niggers we should show them what they get for coming into our territory. We'll beat them back where they belong."

Jimmy said, "way to go! We're going to kick ass tonight." Nick, the poor stutterer just wanted to say, *way to go,* it took him so long that Leo and John just slapped him upside the head, "We know you're in you dumb fuck."

Bob thought, I can't go along with this. This ain't like turning over trashcans, ringing doorbells, shoplifting, stealing on the South Philly market or even a gang fight with fists. This is like revenge for something that might be a rumor. It sounded too pat to be the truth. It sounded like a story made up to cause trouble.

Bob said, "I'm not too sure about this story. It's like all the rumors you ever heard about whites raping colored girls and Negroes raping white girls. It's cross the fence gossip."

John said, "You calling me a liar?"

"No, I'm not. It's just the story sounds fishy."

John said, "Say what you want, you're calling me a liar. I'm glad I dropped your wallet in that store. You mother fucking traitor. I wanted to teach you a lesson, don't break with the gang. We stick together. We are brothers. I see it didn't work."

"Why'd you go and do a thing like that? I could have gone to jail."

"No fucking way. Them Italians got you off. I knew you'd have an alibi. It was just a warning that we'll do even worse if you betray us again with them ginny's or any other fucking body else. Now are you with us or not?" Trapped by the emotions of the previous week, which left him weakened spiritually, and this tough guy with his hands on his shirt almost lifting it out of his pants, the beer swirling in his head, and the loss of Monica, Bob was in a self-destructive state.

"Let go of me John, I'm a member of the gang. Now let me go, I said."

John let go with a shove. "Great to have you back! Let's watch the show."

It was a midget riding a tricycle. He had a crown on his head made of those thin balloons. The clown off to the side was molding the thin balloons into animals for the little kids. When he made them laugh on his bike, he got off for the second part of his show. He was a flame-eating midget who added some tension into the act by executing everything with some ugly, non-poisonous snake around his neck. He wowed the crowd and went up to the tough guys in Bob's gang and made them almost piss themselves by lunging at them with the snake in hand. They cowered like the little kids, the tough guys, that is.

Bob thought, glad that was over. That was too real. John passed out some more beer. They all drank. They were strolling like everyone else, looking down sideshow entrances to see if they were worth the price of admission, when John spotted his prey.

Almost jubilant he said, "Look what we have here! What to my wondering eyes should appear but one, two, three niggers." John led the approach. He called out, "Hey, boys, what are you doing in our neighborhood?"

The boys quickly rose to their feet. They scanned the tightening circle of white around them. John said, "Don't you hear me boys. You wouldn't want to be rude to me in our territory. For the last time, don't you hear me boys?"

Bob wanted to make a run for it. He didn't want to bully people, be a gang member, that had been part of his youthful rebellion. He may have lost Monica, but he didn't lose his mind, his mother, his Grandmom and the possibility of a father. He didn't care if he was a pussy. The drink slowed him down and kept him there a second too long.

Chapter Twelve

Caught off guard and clearly outnumbered, one of the Blacks answered, "We hear you." He couldn't have been much older than twenty. He was thin and lanky; the other two boys were built like halfbacks. The lanky boy spoke again, "Look, we don't want any trouble."

John shot back, "You're damn right you don't want any trouble, you're outnumbered. What about that neighborhood boy and his date you hit on?"

"Man, stop talking shit, no one's been hitting' on any white girl."

John said, "Don't be no wise ass nigger with me. You don't belong here. You're in our territory."

One of the half backs said, "No problem, we'll leave. Just let us through and we'll be out of your territory." The black kids started to move cautiously. The lanky boy was trying to find an opening in the circle, when Jimmy pulled a knife. "You're not getting away so easily."

John shouted, "Way to go, Jimmy!" The two other black kids shouted, "Be careful, Floyd!" In one quick move the black boy knocked Jimmy to the ground and wrested the knife from his hand. Now he was standing brandishing the knife while swiveling his body in a circle at the white boys. Jimmy was yelling, "He sliced me."

Floyd shouted back, "I didn't mean to. I was just defending myself, rules of the street."

His two friends said, "Come on let us go." Jimmy was still yelling about his hand. John said, "You ain't got no rules or rights on this street. You guys ain't going nowhere. "Then he pulled out a gun. A wave of terror pulsed through everyone except Bob. "Put that thing away, you goddam fool. Shoot a gun in the grounds behind the carnival and what are you going to do with the crowd you attract. The place will be crawling with cops. Anyway these guy didn't do anything."

"You calling me a liar? Okay, big guy, get in there and get the knife so we all can go home." Bob hesitated; John brandished the gun for emphasis. "Go ahead Bob, or are you with the niggers? Maybe you can go home with them and see the reception you get in their neighborhood." Bob really had no choice. If he wanted to save himself and this terrorized boy named Floyd, he had to tough it out.

Like a cornered animal, Bob dove at Floyd keeping his eyes and hands focused on the knife. Trying to shake it free of his right hand and blocking with his body, he couldn't loosen this strong boys iron grip. He raised Floyd's knife hand high and kneed him in the gonads and looped his right leg behind and Floyd fell on his back. Bob was on top of him, one hand on the knife hand the other defending himself from Floyd's left. In the struggle they switched positions now Bob was on the bottom protecting himself from the point of the blade. Bob put all his strength in turning away the knife and pointing it toward Floyd. Floyd resisted fiercely. John pointed the gun at the blacks and entered the melee and with the butt of the gun he slammed the right side of Floyd's head, temporarily shifting the advantage to Bob who turned the knife away from himself, inside in the direction of Floyd's chest. Then John took the heel of his foot and rammed it into the small of Floyd's back. The boy collapsed and fell like dead weight on Bob's stomach. Bob wasn't sure who took the hit, him or the black kid. All he knew was, he was drenched in someone's blood. It wasn't until Floyd's eyes looked into Bob's soul that he knew he himself was alive. The boy's eyes looked as if they were about to jump out of their sockets. Bob got out from under and flipped Floyd over. He looked horrified at his and John's handiwork, a blade between the ribs, cutting diagonally in the chest and very probably puncturing the heart.

Bob was in shock. The white kids relaxed their guard. The two other black kids saw their chance and ran for their lives. John raised his gun and was about to unload on them when Bob bowled him over. They were both lucky the gun didn't go off on either one of them. But their luck would run out one-day soon.

Bob found his voice, "Oh my God, what have we done."

"Why didn't you let me shoot the bastards, now they can identify us."

"John," Bob pointed to Floyd, "Isn't one murder enough? How many is your idea of fun."

John said, "What do you want to do, call the priest for the last rites."

Bob said, "No, I think we should get the cops and tell them what happened. It was an accident."

"And your ass is in jail for twenty years. Smart move. Leo, Jimmy, Nick, you go home right now. Stay in today, tomorrow until you hear from me. You were home all night, watched the fights went to bed early and saw and spoke to no one. Take all the back streets and alleys, greet no one and get your asses home and in bed. We'll clean this place up."

Then John looked at Bob's blood stained shirt. "Let's trade. Take your shirt off, roll it up as tightly as you can and give it over to me. Wear mine. I got my tee shirt. With Bob's bloody shirt he extricated with difficulty a knife deeply imbedded on a diagonal in muscle flesh and cartilage. It left the body with a suction noise. Bob's eyes lit up. He saw Floyd blink and his eyes open. "John, he's alive, let's call an ambulance. He has a chance. We didn't kill him." Bob knelt beside the corpse and listened for breath. In the meantime Floyd's eyes had closed and Bob heard a gurgling sound like drowning that he should have recognized but didn't.

John grabbed hold of both of his shoulders, shouting, "Man, get hold of yourself! The guy is dead. He's dead, Bob. Now I'm going home and burning the shirt in the coal heater. I'll drop the knife in the river. You got to get hold of yourself. Do everything I told the other guys to do. You are the biggest risk with your fucking conscience and your guilt. If you blow our cover by talking to anyone, I'll blow you away myself. I may do it anyway, now get the fuck out of here, and don't wimp out on your friends."

Chapter Thirteen

It was close to 10 p.m. when Bob arrived home. John warned him to lay low, not to talk with anyone. He would call Bob in the morning. As he entered the parlor his grandmom called from the kitchen, 'Is that you, Bob?"

"Yes, grandmom."

"Oh, I'm so glad you're home. Do you want a cup of tea?"

He was frightened of any question she might ask, however innocent. Bob had a terrible grimy sweat and he gave off an odor of despair. Controlling himself as best as he could, he didn't want his grandmother to see him in this state. He had something to hide.

"No thank you, grandmom," said Bob.

Coming into the parlor from the kitchen, "What's the matter Bob? You sound upset. You look like you've been in a fight."

"Nothing's wrong, I'm just not feeling well. I think I need to go to bed."

"That's a good idea. Go. Get some rest. If you need me just call."

Bob ran up the stairs. As he lay across his bed with his face buried in the pillow, he cried. He slept fitfully, only to be awakened by the recurring nightmare of Floyd's eyes staring into his, the eyes of the victim, innocent, pleading, defenseless, dead before his time. It seemed like he just managed sleep when his alarm went off.

He was ready to go to work until he realized that he was a murderer. He got up, looked in the mirror and wondered how he could have ever taken a life, how he could face the Pontellos, how he would live another day. All this guilt and the realization that he murdered someone the day after he buried his own mother.

He could hear his grandmother snoring, which made him wonder about his dad. He wondered if his father was at home, if he was sober, if he had indeed changed like he said he did. He walked into the middle bedroom and his father wasn't there.

Monica and her mother were preparing to open up the store. Monica was at the counter when the paperboy arrived with the Philadelphia Daily News.

"Young Man Found Stabbed to Death at Carnival"

A black man about twenty-one years of age was found with knife wounds in his chest. The murder took place in the picnic area of the lake, just behind the Carnival Fair grounds. No witnesses came forward, however, the police believe that there was a witness. They are following a lead.

While Monica was reading her father returned from the waterfront. "I sure could have used Bob's help on the docks today. If your friend isn't back to work by Friday, death or no death, he's going to lose his job."

Mrs. Pontello, who was sweeping the floor, said to her husband, "Dominic, a little patience, the boy just lost his mother." Turning to Monica she said, "Monica, what are you reading so intently?"

"There was a murder last night at the carnival."

Mr. Pontello said, "It's those gangs. Those kids are a menace."

Monica was headed for the kitchen when the phone rang. "Mom, I'll get it back here. Hello!" There was silence. Monica repeated, "Hello!" She could hardly hear the caller. "Could you please speak louder? I can hardly hear you."

"It's me Monica."

"Is that you Bob?"

"Yes!"

"Are you crying? Oh, how stupid of me, of course, you're still mourning your mother."

"Yes Monica, I'm crying."

"Bob, I know it hurts, but everything will be all right."

"I don't think so!"

"What do you mean?"

"Monica, I'm in serious trouble. I don't know what happened to me!"

"Tell me what's wrong."

"I can't talk about it over the phone. Can I see you? Can you come over?"

"It's hard to get away, my parents really need me."

"Please, for just a little while. I have no right to ask this of you, but I don't know where to turn."

Monica hesitated but eventually agreed to meet him within the hour. She wanted to tell her parents or Pasqual, but she knew that they would never approve. Bob sounded so distressed over the phone. She had to meet him at his home.

Her father yelled into the kitchen, "Who was on the phone?"

"Pop, it was a wrong number." After some hesitation, "Pop, can you and mom get along without me today? I'm not feeling well."

"What's wrong Monica? If you feel sick, of course we can get on without you."

"I'm coming down with a sore throat."

Dominic said, "Maybe it's the flu. Don't worry. You go home and rest. We'll take care of the store."

Mrs. Pontello said, "Aunt Theresa will be here any minute. We can manage without you. If you don't nip it in the bud you could be out of work for the better part of a week."

The day was overcast and humid. The weather reports called for thundershowers. She was on the bus to Bob's house and she began to cry. She had never lied to her parents.

Bob was pacing nervously in the kitchen, the smallest room in the house. He had no idea how he would tell Monica. How could he tell her he killed someone? What if she never wanted to see him again? As he was struggling with what to say, the doorbell rang. Monica's eyes narrowed in disbelief when she stared at Bob. His hair looked as if he hadn't combed it in days. It was also apparent that Bob, always so neat in his appearance, hadn't shaved. "Bob, what's wrong," she asked?

As they entered the parlor, Bob shook his head and said, "I don't know where to start."

"Just start from the beginning. My father always says that no matter how serious a problem is, it always looks better after talking about it."

"Not this problem, Monica."

"Bob, I thought you wanted to talk with me."

"I do. I'm sorry, but I need a little more time to get my thoughts together."

"Do you know what I had to do to get here? I lied to my parents. I told them I was sick. This is the first time I've ever lied to them."

"Monica, I'm sorry you had to lie but I am glad you came over. But why did you lie?"

"You sounded like you needed a friend."

"But yesterday, you couldn't wait to get out of here. What would Pasqual say?"

"He wouldn't like it, but I had to come anyway."

Taking her hand as he sat down next to her on the couch he said, "I know you care for me."

Monica noticed a sketch on the coffee table. Placing her hand on her chest she said, "My goodness that looks like me."

"It is you. I planned on giving it to you."

"You drew it?"

"Yes!"

"You have talent."

"I don't know how much talent I have, but I've always loved to draw, especially someone as beautiful as you."

Monica smiled and said, "You surprise me."

"Why is that?"

"You're a romantic guy, and you're a sensitive person."

"What's so surprising about that?"

"The crew you hang with doesn't seem very sensitive. How important are they to you?"

Looking into her eyes Bob said, "You have to understand, Monica that they were there for me when I needed friends. I had lived on Mifflin Street all my life and only had very few friends. But it was John and Leo who reached out for me. I was sitting on the front steps. They came by with a basketball, introduced themselves and told me they lived up the street. We started to hang out, play basketball, touch football and we hung out together. I didn't want to be a loner in my own neighborhood. Like I said, they were there for me."

"I understand your feelings, but you must realize these guys can get you in trouble."

Bob hung his head in shame. He said, "I know, I know you're right." Then he looked up and stared at Monica. Bob's blue eyes fascinated Monica. Their faces slowly moved toward each other until their lips made contact. They kissed passionately. Monica then hung her head shyly giving Bob the opportunity to unbutton her blouse. Her attraction for Bob, whom she loved, overcame her nubile scruples. Then he unfastened her brassiere. Her face was on fire. She covered her breasts with her arms. He caressed her hands softly, reassuringly. Yielding to his tenderness, she lowered her arms. Her beauty overwhelmed him. Bob laid his head against her breasts while Monica wrapped her arms around him.

He thought that he must have been dreaming. Could it be that this beautiful, intelligent girl from a well to do family was interested in him. If this was a dream, Bob didn't want to wake up. This was the first time in his life that he felt truly happy. He loved her from the first day he ever saw her and now they were about to possess one another.

He kissed her breasts and whispered, "Monica, I love you."

"Bob, I love you, with all my heart. I can't run away from you any longer."

She lay back onto the couch and guided him towards her. They remained silent for a few moments looking into each other's eyes.

Bob was about to say something. Monica placed two fingers over his lips and said, "Not now." They kissed repeatedly and made love.

Afterwards, they just lay quietly holding each other. They were lost in a lover's eternity. They lost all concept of time, until the phone rang. Bob struggled to his feet and answered the phone.

"Monica, it's my grandmother. She called to tell me she'd be home within the hour. She was packing up her house. She's putting it up for sale and wants to move in with me and my dad to take care of us."

As they hurried to get dressed Monica turned to Bob and said, "Are you ever going to tell me why you sounded so desperate when you called this morning?"

"Yes, now is the time." Bob walked towards the front window. Looking out toward the street he asked, "Did you hear about the boy that was killed last night at the carnival?"

"Yes, just this morning in the Daily News, you don't have anything to do with that, do you?"

"Monica, it was an accident. We were drinking. John was pushing a fight with those black kids. John ordered me at the point of a gun to take the knife away from the guy. In the struggle we fell. It was an accident."

Monica covered her face with her hands. They were silent for a few seconds. Then Monica lifted her head, pleading, "Bob, you must go to the police."

"They would never believe it was an accident. There were two witnesses. These guys were frightened. We started the trouble. They could say I killed him intentionally."

"You just go and tell the truth."

"I have to think this through."

"There's nothing to think about."

"There's a lot to think about. I could go to jail."

"If these guys get to the police before you do, it'll make you look guilty. Your only hope is to get there and tell the truth."

"They may be too frightened to go to the police. Even if they did, they don't know any of us."

"Bob, you still have to do the right thing."

"I have to talk to John and the guys."

"You have to take care of yourself. It's because of those friends of yours that you are in this mess."

"I can't abandon them. Monica, I need time to think. Please, don't tell anyone."

"Let me tell my Pop!"

"No," shouted Bob.

"But he can help, please Bob!"

"Look the important thing is that *you* believe me. I am no murderer."

"I know you wouldn't hurt anyone on purpose."

"Monica, can you just give me some time. I have to lay low. Listen to the news reports and figure things out. I promise if I can't find any way out of this mess, we could both go to your father and then to the police. It's getting late. You better leave. I'll be in touch with you soon."

Bob walked Monica to the bus station. She didn't want him to take any chances, but he insisted. They were half a block away from the bus stop when they noticed a police car, slowly approaching from behind. Bob's palms were wet, his heart was racing. Monica was shaking, "What shall we do?"

"I'll make a run for it. They won't bother you."

Just as they were about to make a break for it, the patrol car picked up speed and turned the corner. They stopped for a moment and breathed a sigh of relief. Monica was crying. Sweat was dripping down Bob's forehead. He hugged Monica and told her not to worry. After putting her on the bus, he headed home.

Monica hoped to get home before her parents. They followed a predictable routine. Since it was a little after noon when she arrived home, she was safe. And the sickness wouldn't be hard to simulate, because she was heart sick for her lover who was a murderer, accidental or not, ashamed she had lied to her parents, and confused she had betrayed Pasqual and made love for the first time to Bob. She was in love and in fear of losing everything. As Monica placed the key in the door, Aunt Theresa opened it. Monica's eyes widened and her jaw dropped. She threw her arms around her favorite aunt and cried uncontrollably.

"Monica, Monica, you're safe. You're home. I love you sweetheart. What's wrong. Tell Aunt Theresa! I want to help you. It's about Bob, isn't it?" Monica shook her head. "I didn't believe that bull shit about your sore throat. Your mom and dad were so worried, they sent me here to look after you."

"Aunt Theresa, I know you have a lot of questions and I want your advice, but please, not now, I just want to go to my room."

Aunt Theresa let go of her embrace. Monica ran up the stairs to her room. That evening they did not talk. Aunt Theresa would explain to Monica's parents that she was not feeling well and needed her rest. She was, indeed, very sick!

Chapter Fourteen

It was almost eleven p.m. The residents of Mifflin Street had retired for the evening. The outside lights of a few homes were still lit. Those were the homes of the parents who couldn't sleep yet because their teenagers were still on the streets. Bob sat on the stoop with Monica on his mind. How could he have put her in a situation where she disobeyed her parents? He didn't want to lose her, but did he love her enough to let her go? He thought about the boy he had murdered. He glanced at his watch, 11:15, where the fuck was John.

He looked up startled because John was standing in front of him. John spoke first. "This heat sucks." He tore off his T-shirt and draped it over his shoulders.

"Fuck the heat, we got more serious problems."

"We have to run away. There's no other way, Bob."

"No, there must be another way."

"We have to go someplace where no one knows us. Leo thinks like me. The others are still too afraid. We don't need them. Let them stay and face the consequences."

"I don' want to run away and leave my girl. Besides it takes money."

"You're right about the money and there's a lot of it on Ninth Street."

"What do you mean? On Ninth street!"

"All them stores and store owners keeping cash on the premises. We could break in late at night and leave with a shopping bag full of money, enough to tide us over until we can establish ourselves."

"Are you crazy? Do you think it would be that easy?"

"After nine the market is deserted. If we're careful we could be in and out in less than half an hour. All we need is one good score."

"We'd have to know the layout."

"Well, don't you?"

"You don't mean the Pontellos?"

"What better target?"

Bob was hot with anger. "Never in a million years would I steal from them. They're like family."

"Yeah, like family? How well would you think those dagoes would take to an Irish son-in-law. You're deceiving yourself. They can accept your labor, but let you into the family? Never! You know oil and water don't mix."

"John, you're wrong, you gotta be wrong."

"You're just not from the right tribe."

"Just drop it, John, It's not gonna happen."

"Come on, Bob boy, it's me, Johnny. Isn't that why you got the job in the first place, to case the joint, get into the old man's good graces, win his confidence, find out where they hid the cash box, then make your move. I'd say it was pretty slick and now you're gonna tell me you're in love."

"You're a fucking criminal."

"And you're a half-assed saint who's gonna go down. The niggers are going to go to the police, they're going to track us down and you can fry in the chair, not me. You killed a man, you moron, wake up and save your ass!"

"I was trying to take the knife from him. It was an accident. You forced me with a gun."

"Do you think the cops will believe that shit. We're in this together."

"I need time to sort this out. I need to think about what I should do."

Getting up from the steps John pushed his finger deep into Bob's chest, "Listen, if you want to hang around here and go to the chair that's your choice, but I warn you, don't cross me. Don't get in my way, and don't go turning me into the police."

Bob pushed his finger away, "One condition, the Pontello's are off base!"

"Okay for now, but you have to come up with a plan. We need to hit one of those stores on Ninth Street soon. You figure which one. If you don't then it's my call."

63

As John left, Bob realized that the Pontello's were in danger. John was ruthless and would break his word again. Bob went back into the house. His grandmother startled him. She sat in the parlor and stared into space. Bob said, "Grandmom, why aren't you in bed?"

"I couldn't sleep. I heard you talking with someone."

"What did you hear?"

"I don't know exactly, but I figured out you were in some kind of trouble. What's happening? Can I help?"

"Everything's fine, Grandmom. Don't worry. Now you go to bed!"

Mrs. McDermott's eyes darted from her grandson to the picture of her daughter Margaret hanging on the wall. She then turned to Bob and said, "Make sure the front light is on for your mom. She should be home from work shortly. I'm tired. I think I'll go to bed."

Bob lowered his head, weighed down with yet another grief. He reassured his grandmother that he would leave the light on. As he watched her ascend the stairs, he realized how she was always there for him and his mother. Now who would be there for her?

Chapter Fifteen

Maria called to check on Monica. Aunt Theresa assured her that she was fine but needed to rest. She would stay until Maria and Dominic returned home. Maria invited Theresa to stay for dinner. Aunt Theresa accepted but only if she could prepare supper. Maria didn't argue because she knew that once her sister got something in her head, no one could change her mind. Besides she was a great cook.

Maria said, "Theresa, there are some steaks in the freezer."

"Don't worry, I'll put something together."

When the Pontellos arrived home they found dinner prepared and ready to serve. Dominic loved the steak and roasted peppers, especially with crusty Italian bread. Maria was just relieved not to have to cook. "I better call Monica."

"Leave the child rest, Maria! I'm sure she hasn't got much of an appetite. Let's eat first then we can go check in on her." Aunt Theresa wanted to protect her neice's privacy. Nothing could keep Maria from checking in on her daughter. She was half way up the stairs before Theresa could react.

Maria entered the room and found it dark and stuffy. She opened a window a crack and turned on the lamp on the night table. Sitting on the edge of the bed next to her daughter she said, "How are you feeling, Monica?"

Monica turned her head from the pillow and said, "Not well, mom."

"Can I get you anything?"

"Not now." Monica's eyes were so red; her mother couldn't help but notice.

"Is something wrong, honey? Can I take your temperature?"

"No, I don't have a fever." Maria knew something was wrong, just mother's intuition, or maybe the red eyes. She kissed her daughter on the forehead and told her to get some rest, and they would talk later.

During the rest of the night Monica could not sleep. She loved Bob and wanted to spend the rest of her life with him. She was frightened because she could not see how her dream would materialize. Her father would never approve a marriage with an Irish boy. Then there was the tragedy of murder hanging over Bob's head. She began to tremble at the thought of the police hunting down her beloved.

She looked at a white and blue porcelain statue of the Blessed Mother, on the night table. The light her mother had lit was still shining on Mary, Our Lady of Sorrows. Monica was so troubled she couldn't even pray. All she could do was clutch her rosary and squeeze each bead tightly and hope that God would listen to her petitions. She lingered on the crucifix and let the beads fall limply wrapped around her forearm. Sleep came with difficulty.

In the morning, Maria went to check on Monica. She found her sleeping in the chair. She covered her with a blanket and left for the store.

Chapter Sixteen

Bob lay on his back staring at the ceiling unable for the second night in a row to do more than doze off for a few minutes at a time. He told Monica he needed time to think, but he was unable to come up with a plan. Maybe a walk would clear his mind, even though it was still risky to venture out into the public. It was likely by now that the black kids had gone to the police. The police might already be looking for him, equipped with a description. Cooped up in his room, he was stir crazy. To keep his sanity he decided to take the chance that he wouldn't be recognized.

Before leaving he checked in on his grandmother. She was still sleeping. It was early morning when he left his house not sure where he was going. Mostly on side streets and alleys he walked for over an hour until he found himself in front of St. Nicholas Church at Ninth and Tasker. He looked up at the ancient Romanesque façade and decided to enter. In the narthex, Bob blessed himself with holy water and then entered the Church. As he walked up the aisle, his eyes filled with tears. Only a few days ago he accompanied his mother's body up a similar aisle.

It was easy to identify this church as Italian because of the choice of statues lining the walls on both sides of the aisle, St. Francis, St. Anthony, St. Theresa of the Little Flower. In front of each statue were vigil lights. The reflection from these candles were the only illumination in the church, along with the slowly rising sun. It was seven o'clock, an hour before the first Mass of the day would bring in the ancient Italian and Irish women who would pray their rosaries and murmur their prayers before receiving Holy Communion. They would offer their prayers for their wayward sons and husbands, friends with cancer, and for every bit of pain and suffering endured by the human race. Who knew if it wasn't these prayers, which kept the whole human undertaking moving?

Bob turned away from the saints, took a deep breath as his eyes settled upon a life sized crucifix suspended from the ceiling above the altar. Midway between the altar and the communion rail hung the tall red votive light indicating the presence of the Blessed Sacrament.

Bob went immediately to his knees and prayed with a fervor he had never known until now. He begged Jesus to show him the way. His eyes were fixed on the brown, glaring eyes of the Nazarene. There was no answer, just silence, just the agonizing reality of that night at the carnival. The eyes of the crucified reminded him of Floyd. Both sets of eyes seared deeply into his spirit.

Out of the depths of his despair he cried, "God, oh God, help me. What am I going to do?" Just then the sacristy door opened and a priest came out on the altar. Bob thought he had better leave but the kindly priest noticed the boy and called to him. "Son, son, wait a minute! Did you want to talk to a priest?"

"Yes, Father, I would very much like to talk to you, but I wouldn't want to impose on you so early in the morning." The priest had reached Bob, extended his hand and they shook as if to seal a bargain.

"No trouble at all, son. My name is Father Maguire." His warm smile put Bob at ease. "My name is Bob." And Bob wondered if this stranger might not be an answer to his prayer.

Bob told him everything: the murder, compromising Monica with her parents, his sexual encounter, his fear, and his cowardice. He told him of Floyd's eyes and of his inability to sleep. And he asked the most troubling question. "Father, what am I going to do? I have ruined Monica's life and my own, and I have the blood of an innocent man on my hands."

"Bob, it seems to me like you had no intention of killing anyone. However, you must realize that you must face the consequences. And you have to keep in mind that with God there are no hopeless cases."

"Yes Father, but I must decide what the next step is."

"Bob, you know what to do?"

"You mean, turn myself in? How can I do that?"

"Bob, I am giving you the same advice that Monica gave you. That is the only way to take some control over the situation. You have to be willing to perhaps be misunderstood by the police and pray with all of us that the truth will come out. You will have no peace as a fugitive. Better to face manslaughter than throw your entire life away running from yourself. I have to say the eight o'clock Mass. Here's my name and phone number. I want you to tell me where you are, if you are in custody, if you need me for anything. I will not abandon you in your time of need."

The priest blessed Bob and both left: Father to his parishioners and Bob to his uncertain future.

Chapter Seventeen

It was one p.m. and Monica was still asleep in the chair. She probably would have slept away the afternoon had it not been for the phone ringing. On the other end of the line was an impatient Aunt Theresa. Come on Monica; pick up the damn phone she muttered to herself. After the fourth ring Monica answered. "Hello." She was scarcely audible.

"Monica, are you still sleeping?"

"Aunt Theresa, is that you?"

"Who the hell do you think it is, your Irish boy friend?"

"I fell asleep in my chair."

"Well you better get up. It's past lunch time."

"Oh my gosh, I should be at the store."

"Don't worry about the store. Your mother is on her way home to talk to you. She knows something is wrong. You can't hide in your room forever. Now get up and prepare yourself. Get ready to tell all."

"I'll try Aunt Theresa."

"Try my ass. You face your problems like an adult or they will consume you. I'm praying for you honey, don't let yourself down."

"Okay, okay, you're right. I've got to be strong. You pray and I'll freshen up like you said." As she headed for the shower she heard the front door open. "Mom, is that you?"

"Yes, honey, can we talk?"

"Let me shower first, I won't be long. Could you make us a cup of tea?"

"I'll be in the kitchen. When you're ready, come down and we can talk over tea."

Monica knew she had to confide in her mother. She was not good at lying or at any other kind of subterfuge. As she showered and dressed, she almost looked forward with relief to the prospect of sharing her burdens with a loving mom.

Maria was putting some milk and sugar in her cup when Monica entered the room. "There you are, sit down. Are you feeling any better, Monica?"

"A little. I don't know what time it was when I finally dozed off. Thanks for the blanket."

"You're welcome, honey." Mrs. Pontello placed a cup of tea in front of her daughter.

"Why are you home so early?"

"I was worried about you. Your father and Aunt Theresa are taking care of the store. We are all worried. We all know something is up. You only have to talk to me, if you want. Tell me, honey, where were you yesterday? What happened?"

"I was with Bob."

Mrs. Pontello pushed her cup to the side. "Were you with him the whole day?"

Monica hesitated. She knew this was the moment of truth. "Yes, at his house. His grandmother was out."

"What happened?"

Monica remained silent as she picked at a paper napkin on the table. "Mom, I don't know how to tell you this."

"Just tell me, you know I love you."

"I can't."

"I think I can guess what happened." Monica's face turned beet red. She told her what happened between her and Bob. However, she mentioned nothing about the carnival. Mrs. Pontello listened and kept silent. Then she spoke. "I am disappointed in your behavior but I love you dearly." By this time Monica had her arms around her mother's neck and was crying like a baby.

"Mom, I'm so ashamed of myself. I must have hurt you deeply."

"What does this mean about your engagement to Pasqual."

"Mom, I love Bob like I've never loved anyone before."

"Monica, I told you so many times when you were growing up that an attraction to someone doesn't necessarily mean love."

"Mom, it's more than just a physical attraction. This is the real thing."

"I just don't want you throwing your life away."

"Mom, I know I let you and Pop down, but I can't marry Pasqual after being with Bob."

"What kind of future will you have with him? He and his family are poorer than church mice."

"I honestly don't even know if we have a future."

"Well, then, don't jump into anything. Give it time! Lead with your head this time, not your heart."

"When I first met Bob I was attracted to him. I didn't want to admit it. I can't explain why I love him. I didn't ask to fall in love with him, it just happened."

"You know your father will never approve of Bob. He thinks he is a good worker and he likes him, but I am sure he doesn't want him as a son-in-law. You know what he always says, about oil and water not mixing. There are ethnic differences, you know."

"Bob being Irish and Pop's objections are not the only obstacles."

"What do you mean?"

Taking her teacup to the sink Monica answered, "I mean there are other things that could keep us apart."

"Like what? Don't make me guess!"

"Mom, not now, please not now. Give me time, please!"

Not wanting to push too much Maria decided to back down. "Okay, Monica, you need time. Pop will be home for supper, then you'll have to talk with the two of us."

"I can't face Pop."

"Monica, he loves you as much as I do. You can't run away from him. You'll always be his little girl." Monica was sobbing uncontrollably now. "Honey, if you want to be alone with your feelings, go to your room and I'll call you for supper. But for heaven's sake, think about what's good for you and not about pleasing or disappointing us. You are our whole life. We don't want anything to happen to you."

Monica shook her head quickly like a little girl and went silently to the privacy of her own room.

Mr. Pontello arrived home promptly at seven. Maria was in the kitchen putting the finishing touches on supper. Dominic greeted her with a kiss. "Maria, I could smell the sauce as soon as I came in the door. You're still the best."

"No need for flattery, you're going to be fed." Dominic laughed and asked about Monica.

"She needs to talk with you."

"What happened, is she all right?"

"No, but she'll be fine as soon as her daddy helps her." She then proceeded to tell him what had occurred between Monica and Bob. The news was not taken well. He paced the kitchen floor cursing in Italian. Mrs. Pontello begged him to take it easy. "It happened and there is nothing we can do about it."

"Maria, I don't want to hear that. I trusted that Irish bastard and look what he did to our daughter. She's not going to ruin her life."

"Dominic, remember our daughter will be twenty-one in a few months. This is Nineteen-Fifty-Six. Times are changing. You cannot force her to marry someone she doesn't love."

"All of a sudden she doesn't love the man she is engaged to. This guy turned her head with his good looks and a line of flattery. She could just drop this interloper and marry Pasqual and things will go back to the way they were."

"Don't you understand, Dominic, it's not that easy? She told me she really cares for Bob. She says it's different than her feelings for Pasqual. She realized she can't marry him after she has been with Bob."

"I won't hear any more of it."

"Dominic, you must listen and keep an open mind."

"Never, never!" He shouted.

"Our daughter needs us."

"I told you, Maria, I don't want to hear anymore of this."

"Do you want to lose our daughter? Do you want that to happen?"

73

Dominic quieted down, pulled out a chair and sat down. He remained silent. Maria continued to advise him. "Maria, what's happening to our world? Things are changing so fast. There was a time when Italians would only marry Italians. It was important to maintain our traditions. My only hope was that Monica would marry a fine man, an Italian, who was interested in our business. The Pontello tradition has always been to hand down their businesses to their sons."

"I could not give you a son. I am sorry, Dominic."

"Oh Maria, I'm not angry with you. We both wanted more children. We thanked God we had Monica and went on with our life. My dream stayed alive in Monica. It would be through our daughter and a son-in-law that we could continue the family tradition. And now this Irish boy is trying to force himself into our family."

"Dominic, listen to yourself! You're talking about your dreams. What about Monica's dreams?"

"Monica had hopes for the business. Yes, I had dreams, but they were for Monica as well."

"I know you mean well, Dominic. You want the best for her. So do I."

"Monica's not thinking clearly. We didn't raise her to sleep around."

Maria snapped. "Monica did not sleep around. I don't want to hear those words coming from your lips, her father. I am hurt as much by this as you are. It happened and we will not resort to name calling and innuendo. We both love her and we will stand by her. She made a mistake but Monica is a good girl."

"Do you expect me to act as if nothing has happened?"

"I expect you to stand by your daughter. All your talk of tradition, it's also part of our tradition to stand by our children and help them when they are in need."

"Yes, we should stand by Monica, but that does not mean we approve of her ruining her life. She must give this boy up."

Monica had been listening the entire time from her bedroom. She had hoped to avoid a confrontation with her father, but her fear of losing Bob gave her the courage to leave her bedroom. "No!" said Monica, "As she entered the kitchen. Pop, I am sorry for disappointing you, but I can't apologize for falling in love with Bob."

"Love, what do you know about love. A week ago you were in love with Pasqual. Now you're in love with this character. It doesn't take much to get you to use that word."

"I know you are angry, but I love Bob. The love I had for Pasqual was not the same. I won't marry Pasqual."

"I will do everything in my power to keep you from making a fool of yourself."

"What do you mean?"

"You heard me. If you don't stop this foolishness, then I'll stop it. I'll take care of Bob O'Connor myself." Dominic stormed out of the house. Monica ran after him screaming, "Pop, Pop!"

Dominic had disappeared for most of the night. Maria was on the phone. She called Theresa, some of Dominic's friends. No one had heard from him. She even called the store thinking he might be there but there was no answer.

Monica was pacing the parlor floor worried about her Dad and Bob. Even though there was no answer at the store, Monica had an intuition that her father was there. They grabbed their coats and headed for Ninth Street.

Chapter Eighteen

Bob glanced over at the couch. His grandmother had fallen asleep watching "I Love Lucy," her favorite TV show. The Philadelphia Daily News was on the floor next to the couch. The headlines grabbed his attention. *Floyd Brown killed at Carnival Grounds, buried today.* Then in smaller print, *survived only by his mother.* Bob felt the tension in his entire body. He had to control himself from shaking when he read that two eyewitnesses were being questioned. That probably meant that Floyd's two friends had gone to the police, or somehow the police found out about them.

He gently woke his grandmother and helped her to bed and turned off the TV.

In the silence he recalled his visit earlier in the day to St. Nicholas Church. Bob believed in his heart that it was no accident that he met Father Andrew McGuire. He didn't want to go to jail but knew in his heart of hearts that Monica and Father Maguire were right. He would never know happiness if he didn't pay for the consequences of his actions. Who would take care of grandmom if he went to jail? His only hope was his father. He decided to go and look for him.

As Bob opened the front door, John greeted him. "Hey, where are you going so late?"

Leo said, "I guess you were coming to look for us."

"Yeh, Leo! Hi, John."

"Is your grandmom out of the way?"

"Yes, Leo, she's asleep." John pushed past Bob into the house and Leo followed. He said, "We got to talk."

Bob glared at the two of them and said, "We can't talk too loud and wake my grandmother up."

"We got to make our plans. Leo and I saw the Daily News and we can't have more than a couple of days before they nab us. We have to get out of town, and we need money fast."

"Don't panic, John."

"Did you hear me, they got two witnesses. Floyd's friends can describe us and then the police will be all over us. And the rest of the gang is in hiding. They are all chicken, and it wouldn't take much for one of them to turn us in to save their own skin."

"My grandmother's sick, I can't leave her."

"Bob, are you for real? What are you a fucking nursemaid? Get your head out of your ass. You might die in the chair. Too much talk, it's over." John banged his fist on the coffee table and said, "We hit the Pontellos tonight."

"I told you to leave them alone."

"You never had problems hitting any stores in the past."

"This is different. I don't do burglary anymore."

"With or without you we are going to hit the Pontellos' store and any others on the street we take a notion to do." John got up from the sofa and looked Bob in the eye. "I had it with you. I don't care if you come or not. But I'm warning you, stay out of our way. Well, why the stares, got anything to say?"

Bob thought if he went he could minimize the damage and, in the unlikely event that a Pontello was there, he could help avoid violence. "I'm in!"

"That's the spirit, Bob. I knew you were one of us." Then Leo put his arm on Bob's shoulder and said, "Now you're talking sense."

"Bob, where do they keep the cash?" asked John.

"In the register!"

"No kidding," said John. You know what I mean, no secret safe, no movable floor boards?"

"No nothing like that, maybe a little petty cash in the drawer of the kitchen table. No safe!"

"Well we'll start there and maybe along the way we'll make a bigger hit. Then we'll get out of town. Those wops are sneaky; they always have a hidden stash of money they don't tell no one about, not their kids, not the government. We'll find out their dirty little secrets and then get out of town."

"I'm in, but no one gets hurt, no guns, no beatings."

"You think we're crazy? We don't want to add to the charges already against us," said John.

Bob went to the bottom of the stairs to listen for his grandmother's snoring. Satisfied she was asleep, and knowing he would turn himself into the police after his friends left town that night, "Let's go!"

John said, "Let's be quick about it. Ninth Street here we come!"

Chapter Nineteen

Maria and Monica arrived at the store just as the bells of St. Peter's sounded eleven. It was dark and the streets were deserted. As they had guessed, Dominic was sitting behind the counter, his eyes red with crying.

Maria had thought her husband had drunk too much wine. "Dominic, are you all right?" He was silent. Maria then cursed in Italian to no one in particular and said, "We've been married over thirty years and now I get the silent treatment. It won't work. Answer me now, are you okay? Have you been drinking?"

"No, I'm not all right and no, I haven't been drinking, although I should have. You know what I was thinking of doing?"

"How could we know anything? You ran out of the house like a mad man."

"Pop, I understand how you feel."

"Do you, Monica? I'm angry, angrier than I have ever been in my entire life. I'm sitting here thinking I can still go over to Bob's house and warn him to stay away from you. If he refuses I thought of going to the mob to have his legs broken. That's how angry I am."

"Dominic, how can you talk that way? We got this far in life without help from them, and in your maturity you are going to them to settle a personal score. That's not the moral man I married. If you are serious, then you have gone mad."

He put his face in his hands and tried to hold back the tears. "Maria, It's not me. That's why I'm still here trying to sort it all out."

"Pop, I'm sorry for hurting you and causing all this pain. I love you, but I can't undo what's done. Please don't hate Bob. I am just as much to blame. I went to him willingly."

Maria excused herself to make some coffee and to leave father and daughter alone to heal.

"But you are my daughter. I had dreams for you. This business would be yours and your husband's. Your accounting expertise and a man willing to work hard for you and his family, it was a simple dream, a good living, a good marriage and plenty of children to take your place when the time came. Ninth Street can go on forever."

"Pop, you and mom have given me a wonderful life. I am sure I could have the same dreams for my children, but I want to live those dreams with Bob, not with Pasqual. I can't say for sure what will happen between Bob and me because Bob has severe problems, but I do know that I can't marry Pasqual. I feel secure and safe with him, but that's not enough. Over the years I've seen the love you and mom had. It is still like it was when you met, or at least like the stories you told about your first meeting."

"Monica, they were no stories. They were the truth." Dominic lit up as he retold of his first meeting with Maria. "Your mother came into the store looking for a job. I looked her up and down. I stared and couldn't take my eyes off of her waist length brown hair, hazel eyes and olive complexion. She was the most beautiful girl in the world. When she agreed to marry me two months after we worked together so well in the store, I was the envy of Ninth Street." Dominic took his daughter's hand. "Monica, you look so much like your mother. I had very little money when I started out, but with your mom at my side we prospered. She never complained. You know your mother never cared if I were a businessman or a laborer. She would have been at my side regardless. Our love sustained us and even made us wealthy."

"Dad, I don't want to anger you, but that is exactly what I have with Bob. Your marriage had nothing to do with security or business. You and mom are lucky to have one another. Pasqual is a great guy, but we never had that kind of love."

"You know in the old country marriages were arranged among families by parents. Many found romance even under those unpromising situations. There are as many roads to love as there are roads to Rome."

"Daddy, are you even listening to me?"

"I hear you. So this is the love you found with Bob."

"I love him and he loves me, but I am afraid we will never marry?"

"Monica, this doesn't make any sense. Why can't you marry him?"

"I promised Bob I wouldn't tell anyone what his problem was."

From the kitchen Maria called. "Coffee's ready!" When Maria was pouring Dominic noticed her fingers as they gripped the handle of the coffeepot. There were bruises, broken flesh healed and scarred, split fingernails, all the wounds from opening too may crates of produce. He felt guilty he hadn't given her an easier life. Weary from too much emotion they sat and drank in an almost dazed silence. Only the bells of St. Peter tolling midnight roused them and the strange sounds coming from the front of the store.

John took a long screwdriver from his back pocket while Leo stood look out. Maria cried, "Dominic, call the cops! Someone is breaking in."

"You and Monica stay here and call 911, and I'll go out and greet our guests. He took hold of a baseball bat leaning by the door. Usually break-ins on the market were not armed robbery, just punk kids looking for some easy cash.

"Please, Pop, don't go into the store. Wait for the police."

"Dominic, don't go!"

"Don't worry."

Dominic quietly entered the darkened store with the bat in hand. He saw what he was sure was Bob and some strangers. He threw on the light. "Get away from that register!" They suddenly turned towards Dominic. John's fingers were still in the register with Leo holding the cash bag. Bob stood beside them. "So, Bob, you planned on robbing me all along."

"I didn't, Mr. Pontello"

"Well, what the hell is this? I gave you a job and this is how you repay me."

81

"I couldn't stop them. I came along to make sure no one got hurt."

When Monica heard Bob's voice she ran out of the kitchen. "Bob, you're not robbing my parents, are you?"

Maria ran after her and screamed at the intruders, "Get out right away, the cops are coming." When she saw Bob, "You, Bob! You love my daughter and you break into our store?"

"I can explain everything. It's not what you think, Mrs. Pontello."

"I can only think what my eyes tell me. I think my husband was right about you all the time."

John had had enough. "Enough of this family crap. What is this? Family night at church! Listen old man, if you want your family left alone, drop the bat and give us all your cash, here and in the back. You wops always have a secret stash. I want it all." Then he pulled out a 45 from his back pocket. "I mean it, move, and fast, the cops are coming!" Then he laughed cynically because he had just quoted Mrs. Pontello's empty threat.

"No guns, I told you, no one gets hurt." Bob asserted himself.

"Bob, be a good little boy and tell Papa Pontello to put the friggin' bat down, or I'll shoot it out of his hand."

"Mr. Pontello, please put the bat down. No one's going to get hurt." Reluctantly he put the bat down. Leo feverishly filled the bag with the stolen cash. Maria said to Bob, "Why are you involved with them?"

Bob told John and Leo, "Just take the money and get out."

John said, "Oh, Mr. Innocence and Light. Did you tell them about what happened at the Carnival?"

"You shut up, John!" John laughed and Leo urged John to hurry. The police were coming. "We got plenty of time. Bob, family friend, ask the old man where the hidden stash is."

Mr. Pontello said, "Get out, you got what you came for. There is no hidden stash."

"Oh, its going to be fun taking care of you, old man, you and your contempt for us low life criminals."

"What are you saying, John?"

"You know exactly what I am saying. There is no way we can let these people go."

"You're not going to hurt anyone."

"And who's going to stop me."

Dominic had his arms around Maria and Monica in a move to protect them. It was a useless ineffective protection but an instinctual reaction. Bob said, "I'll stop you."

"I'd like to see you try. Are you acting like *you* never killed anybody?"

Dominic looked at Maria then at Monica who had her eyes fixed on Bob. "What's he saying, Bob?" Dominic asked, as if things were getting clearer.

"Tell him Bob, what are you waiting for?" John asked with a malevolent smile "It was an accident, I didn't mean to kill anyone."

Leo interrupted, "John, we better leave."

Mrs. Pontello told them once again, "You better get out. The police are on their way."

Leo said, "Please John, let's get out of here."

"All of you shut up. It's a bluff." He moved his gun from one hand to the other. John was sweating. Bob knew he was on the edge. Bob said, "John, take the money and leave while you still have the chance."

"It's not so easy. They can identify us. They have to go."

"No, you can't, John." Bob said.

"John, just let them go, I got the bag with the money. There's a lot of money in the bag."

"You wimp. You want to go to jail? Take the change too!"

Bob was standing at John's side. "John, how much you think you got in the bag."

"I don't know but it's a start."

"How much is there, old man?"

"Count it yourself you son-of-a-bitch." John was aiming at Mr. Pontello's head. Bob grabbed John's arm forcing him to point the gun in the direction of the ceiling. A shot went off. Leo

83

dropped the moneybag. Mr. Pontello grabbed the bat and went for Leo's kneecaps bringing him to the floor. Bob and John were struggling for the gun. John broke loose and hit Bob across the face with the gun, sending him to the ground. "Old man, I'm going to enjoy filling you with holes." John lowered the gun in Dominic's direction who was crouched in front of the flower case. Dominic said, "You'll never get the big money, you bastard."

John unloaded a second shot at the freezer. He missed his huddled target and hit the overhead sign, *A Rose on Ninth Street*. Bob recovered enough to pounce on John. Mr. Pontello was beside Bob and John with his bat ready to disarm John. It was too late. The gun discharged and Bob fell off John. Dominic didn't miss the opportunity to give him a shot to the head and to bludgeon the hand with the gun. If John wanted to shoot he couldn't. Mr. Pontello intended to break every bone in that murderous hand and succeeded.

In the meantime the police had arrived. Maria rushed to lead them into the burglarized store. Monica ran to Bob. He had difficulty speaking and his shirt was drenched with blood. All he could say was Monica's name. Monica told him not to talk and that the rescue squad had been called. She held his hand. "Bob, everything is going to be fine." She feared the worst. Maria and Dominic drew closer to their unlikely deliverer and heard him say, "Monica, I love you. I am sorry about everything. Forgive me!"

"Bob, I love you too. Now just rest, save your energy, help is on the way."

"Monica, tell your parents everything. They have a … right…. to…know…" And he passed out.

When the medics arrived Monica didn't want to let go but they were persistent and knew their job. Maria and Dominic both embraced their daughter.

Monica told them everything. It was one of those instances where knowledge and happiness were as far as the east is from the west. Now everyone was distraught and completely miserable.

Chapter Twenty

The detective in charge informed Dominic that he would not be able to open the store for business until the investigators had completed their job. He estimated that it would take most of the day. Dominic looked on as one detective retrieved the bullets, another gathered fingerprints and a uniformed police officer had blocked off the puddle of blood next to the cash register.

Maria and Monica were in the kitchen. The family had been at the store the entire night, resting from time to time on the kitchen table. Monica was too overwhelmed to rest. Her mother comforted her. "You can't lose faith now, Monica. He's young, in good health and he loves you. He is in good hands. The doctors know what they are doing."

"Mom, you have to take me to the hospital."

"If that's what you want, that's what we'll do. But on the way I want to stop by Bob's house and tell his grandmother and father what happened. I'll do all the talking. You just get yourself together. Dominic! Dominic, we need you in the kitchen."

"What is it Maria, they need me out there."

"You can't let go, can you. They don't need you to do their police work. Get the car we're going to the hospital but on the way we have to tell Bob's father and grandmother what happened. I am sure they'll want to go with us to the hospital."

When they pulled up in front of Jim O'Connor's house the sun was just about ready to rise. They found him sitting on the front stoop. His head was resting in his hands. He didn't even hear the Pontello's approach. Mrs. Pontello had to call his name twice before he responded he slowly raised his head. "Do I know you? Yes I do. You own the produce store on Ninth Street where Bob works. One of the owners, that woman with the broom chased me away and now you want to talk to me."

"Mr. O'Connor, please understand, we were running a business and Theresa, my sister has to be on her toes about who she lets into the store. We're…"

"Mom, enough already, we're wasting time. It's about Bob, Mr. O'Connor."

"What did my son do?"

"He's seriously hurt and in the hospital with a gun shot wound."

"Hurt," he repeated as he straightened up. Even though he was intoxicated he understood what Monica had said. Mrs. Pontello proceeded to tell Mr. O'Connor the recent events that lead to his son's hospitalization.

"My God, my poor boy!"

Mr. Pontello said, "We'll take you and Mrs. McDermott to the hospital. You'll have to break the news to her. We'll wait in the car. If you don't think she can take the stress, let her sleep."

"No, I think she'll want to be there if there is anything wrong with her grandson."

They waited a half an hour until finally a confused and crying grandmother emerged from the house and got into the back seat of Mr. Pontello's roomy Buick Roadmaster. The two men rode up front, according to custom.

The hospital was a five minute drive the other side of Broad Street. As early as it was, the waiting room of St. Agnes hospital was filled to capacity. Monica found granny a seat and Mr. O'Connor sat on the floor next to her. Monica sensed that it would be a long wait. Her father and mother, always the thoughtful host and hostess went to get coffee and Danish at the machines in the nearby lobby. Monica approached the desk and asked Nurse Nelson, whose name was conspicuously displayed on top her counter, "How is Bob O'Connor doing?"

"He's lost a lot of blood but he has been transfused. I believe they will start operating on him shortly, now that they are sure he is ready for whatever procedures he has to endure. He is doing remarkably well for someone who has sustained such a serious injury. The doctors will come out and report to the family any new developments. You just have to hold tight, honey. It's a waiting game. Try not to make it worse than it has to be. I don't have to tell you, but you can pray here or down the hall, where there is a chapel. That's all we can do, honey, at this point. I have seen people come here in worse condition than your Bob, and they have walked out of here hale and hearty."

Mr. O'Connor half heard Monica's words with Nurse Nelson. He looked up at Gloria McDermott and said, "Our boy is in trouble."

"God help him, Jim!"

"Gloria, I haven't been a father to my son."

"Well, its time to change all that."

"Gloria, I want to thank you."

"For what?"

"In all the years I knew you, never once did you criticized me. I know I was a failure as a husband and a father."

"Regardless of whatever weaknesses you had, Margaret idolized you. I never wanted to come between a man and his wife and the way she loved you."

"It may be hard to believe but I really loved Margaret. She was the best thing that ever happened to me. I just regret that I didn't show my love more. I hope she knew."

"She always believed that someday you would give up drinking. Margaret had a lot of hope. Hope in you. Hope in God. She knew you loved her." Jim smiled at these last words. The Pontellos had returned with the coffee. Trying to cool off this machine-heated beverage helped pass some of the stressful waiting time. Finally a bespectacled physician with wire-rimmed glasses perched precariously half way down his nose came out to speak with the family and friends of Bob.

"Hello, my name is Dr. Hand. I am a cardiologist and I am assisting at this operation. Bob has been stabilized and is ready for the next step. The bullet has lodged near his heart. Of course, we must surgically remove the bullet. No major arteries have been compromised. But any operation near the heart is by definition delicate. His youth and successful transfusion of lost blood has put him in a better position for a successful outcome. If anything major develops, we will send word to you during and after the operation. Please be patient and hopeful. Prayers and patience will carry the day. At this point Bob is conscious and stable. Nurse Nelson informed him that all of you were here. He smiled and dictated this name and number with a short message, which he asked Monica to take care of when she sees fit. We will do our best and so will Bob. He's a very brave boy."

Monica opened the dictated note:

"Monica, I will get through this operation because I want to see your beautiful face again. I love you from the bottom of my heart. This is Father McGuire's phone number. I met him early yesterday morning before the eight o'clock mass. He told me to call him anytime I needed him. Monica, I need him today. Would you bring him to me?"

Monica had her work cut out for herself. She told her father about the priest. Mr. Pontello said that he would return to the store and wait for Monica's call. Then he would pick up Father McGuire. Mr. Pontello was not the kind of person who could sit still and wait in a hospital room when there was a chance he could get the store up and running as soon as the police were finished. He would call upon that old workhorse, Aunt Theresa. They would put this ugly incident behind them in short order.

Chapter Twenty-one

The early morning edition of the Inquirer had just been delivered to the business establishments on Ninth Street. Dominic's friends and fellow merchants would soon learn of the family's near brush with death just hours ago and of the courageous and successful attempt of their employee Bob O'Connor to rescue them. No sooner had Dominic returned to the store to find out that the police would finish their work by midday. Dominic decided he needed the extra time to get the store in shape so he let the sign stay: Closed, due to an emergency, Will reopen tomorrow morning at seven.

This was the first time in thirty-years that Pontellos would not be open. Even when there was a death in the family, a worker or a distant relative would keep the stand running. Dominic returned from the hospital ready to roll his sleeves up and work around the police. To do that he had to call Theresa who lived five blocks away. There was work to be done: the front door had to be repaired, the bullet holes puttied and painted and the floor scrubbed with pine oil. Theresa was about to leave for work when the phone rang. "Who the hell could that be so early in the morning? Hello!"

"Theresa?"

"Dominic?"

"Yes. I wanted to catch you before you got to the store. I don't want you to get upset. Everything is okay."

"Well, I'm upset. What the hell happened?"

"Bob's friends broke into the store and Maria, Monica and I were in the kitchen and they were armed."

"Sant' Antonio, those bastards!"

"Listen, Theresa. Bob saved our liveds He was shot and in serious condition."

"My God, is everyone all right?"

"Monica and Maria are at St. Agnes with Bob's dad and grandmother."

"I'm on my way."

"Theresa, we can't open today. The store is in shambles. We have a lot of work to do to get ready to open tomorrow."

"Don't worry, Dominic! We'll get it done. You and me at the store and Maria and Monica at the hospital! Everything will work out. See you."

Just as he hung up the phone a voice called out from outside the storefront. "Yo, Dominic, you in there?"

It was the president of the Ninth Street Merchant's association, Carl Rosato. Dominic walked to the front of the store, opened the front door and stepped outside. There he greeted his long time colleague with a hearty handshake. "Carl, thanks for coming by."

"Dominic, I read what happened in the morning newspaper. Is everyone okay?"

"Everyone is fine except Bob. He is in surgery now for removal of a bullet that could have killed me or my wife and daughter. It was a close call. When he recovers it'll just be a bad dream. They already have the perpetrators in custody."

"Dominic, if you need a short term loan or some muscle, we'll get the money and help you almost immediately."

"Thanks a lot, Carl. But that won't be necessary. My sister-in-law and me can manage it. If I need you I'll know where to call. Thanks again,"

"Nothing at all, Dominic. We have to be good to one of our oldest establishments. After all where would we be without Pontello's produce."

Dominic saw things a little differently after that act of kindness. He genuinely thought that everything would turn out all right and he and his family and Bob would all wake up from this nightmare.

Chapter Twenty-two

Monica's eyes looked at the clock as if it were about to explode at some horrible moment in her imagination. The rest waited quietly, but nervously, for the surgical door to open into the hospitality room. Both Maria and Monica felt this was the end of Bob. Grandmom just had enough energy to finger her rosary beads, murmuring over and over "Hail Mary, full of grace..." Bob's Dad, Jim, was full of remorse and guilt. He stood leaning on one of the double doors, looking into the windows and catching nothing but a glare. His eyes glazed over and he went semi-conscious and brought himself back to Christmas Eve, a long time ago.

Little Bobby was upset, because his father was going to Murphy's bar. He pleaded with him to stay home. "I'll be back, son. I am just going to wish some friends a Merry Christmas."

"You won't be back tonight."

"Sure I will, son."

"Dad, please stay home. I need you to help me set up the trains."

"I will. I promise. Margaret, tell him I'll be back."

"Do you have to go, Jim?"

"Margaret, you know I'll be back. Trust me, son." And Jim was like he was drenched in regret. Why didn't I stay? I left too often and now my boy is going to leave me. How can I ever make it up to him?

He was roused from his reverie by a portly nurse tapping with her nails on the glass window, anxious to get out of the surgical corridor but Jim was in the way. She had news for the family.

"Bob is still in surgery. They are not sure when it will be over, but I assure you it will be soon. And Dr. Hand will report to you and answer all of your questions."

In the meantime, Monica had called Father Maguire and offered to have her father pick him up. He declined, preferring the flexibility of his own car. As the nurse was going back into the surgical wing, Father Maguire entered the hospitality room. He had a gentle presence. His white pearly teeth complemented his well-groomed silver hair. He explained to Grandmom and Jim how he met Bob yesterday and enjoyed a pleasant conversation at St. Nicholas Church, just before the eight o'clock Mass. "Then I gave him my name and phone number and asked him to call if he ever needed me. I was so happy when Monica called and that Bob wanted to speak with me. But I am deeply troubled by his need for surgery. Is there any word on his condition?"

Jim said, "Nothing to report yet, Father. He is still in surgery."

"Well, I guess there's nothing left to do but pray."

"I'm ashamed to say I don't know any prayers. I've fallen away from the Church."

"Mr. O'Connor, just pray from your heart. Say whatever is in your heart."

"Father, would you lead us in prayer," said Mrs. McDermott.

"I'd be happy to. Dear God, be with Bob in this time of need. Guide his doctors and help us to comfort each other. I ask you this in your son Jesus' name. May everything be done according to your will. Amen."

Mrs. McDermott began to cry hysterically. "First my daughter, now my little grandson. His eyes are so much like his mother's. I know the Lord is going to take him like he took my daughter."

"I know you are in pain. There is nothing I can say to ease your pain except that God will take care of Bob. Whatever happens, he will take care of him. God love's your little grandson as much as you do."

Suddenly the doors opened into the hospitality room and Dr. Hand was ready with his report. "I am happy to tell you that Bob survived the operation. He had a lot of damage around the heart muscle. We removed the bullet and have succeeded in halting the excessive bleeding. He was transfused already and should receive another transfusion in the recovery. The next hours are crucial because of the possibility of infection. Because of that risk, his prognosis is guardedly optimistic. That means we think he will make it barring any unforeseen complications."

What wasn't told the family was a phenomenon, which was just becoming more commonly known. Certain hospitals carried infections in certain rooms, in the walls, on the floor, no one knew for sure, but many hospitals infected their own patients. Who knew if this hospital had its own intractable bacteria or virus, or if the air itself would do Bob in? Bob was in the desert where it was him, his body and his Maker.

Chapter Twenty-three

Most of the repairs had been completed. Soon the attempted robbery would all be history, if only Bob would get better quickly. Dominic had just sanded the front door. Theresa was putting the finishing touches on the floor. The room was filled with the fresh scent of pine oil.

It was nearly three and they had worked through lunch. Theresa thought it was time for a break. "Dominic, there's some cheese and bread in the kitchen. How 'bout I make a pot of coffee and a couple of sandwiches?"

"Make something for yourself, Theresa, I'm not hungry."

"No matter, Dominic, you got to keep up your strength." The clanging of the trolley drew Dominic to the window. He peeked through the blinds. "Dominic, every time you look out the window when those damn bells clang, your see the same street and the same trolley. Nothing's changed since the last time you looked."

"It's busy out there, Theresa."

"It's busy every day except Sunday!"

"I miss not being open. I like being part of the action."

"Dominic, we'll be reopen tomorrow. Anyway the store needed a good cleaning anyway."

"Oh my God, Theresa, here comes Pasqual. I can't face him. I don't know what to say."

"Go out and buy the lock for the front door at the hardware store and use the back."

"Thanks, Theresa! I hope he's gone by the time I get back." As Dominic exited through the rear, Theresa opened the front door. "Hello, Pasqual, how are you?"

"Theresa, I'm a wreck. I'm worried sick about Monica, and I haven't seen her in a few days."

"Come in, come in, we'll talk inside."

"Where is she?" As he said this, his eyes darted around the store as if she was about to appear any moment.

"She's at the hospital with Maria waiting for news about Bob."

"Theresa, I read all about it in the Inquirer. Where is Mr. Pontello?"

"He had to buy a lock for the front door."

"I don't want to lose her, Theresa but I know she loves him. I never wished harm on anyone but today I found myself wishing Bob would die. God forgive me. I really don't want that to happen."

"Pasqual, you're angry and in love. I understand your feelings."

"Theresa, I'm furious. I love Monica with all my heart. There is nothing I wouldn't do for her. I can't bear the thought of losing her."

"I understand, Pasqual. Sit down I want to talk with you."

"We were happy until that creep came along and turned her head." Pasqual put his face in his hands and began to cry. "I just can't live without her, Theresa." Theresa put her hand gently on his shoulder, "Pasqual, your heart is broken. That's what happens when you love someone and they don't love you back."

"But she did love me once."

"Yes, Pasqual, and there are many kinds of love. I know. My heart was broken once."

"You?"

"Yes, me! What do you think, I was born with gray hair and wrinkles? I was madly and passionately in love. I was eighteen years old when my parents arranged my marriage. He was a fine man, Vincent DeMarco. We knew each other from childhood.

We both shared the dream of someday leaving Sicily for America. He adored me and I loved him. Then one day a neighbor and a friend of the family, Mr. Roselli visited us and brought his nephew Antonio Greco along. Antonio was spending the summer with his uncle. When our eyes met, my heart melted. We did not take our eyes off one another the entire evening. Several times we managed to meet in secret that summer. I tried to explain to my parents that I loved Antonio, but they wouldn't hear of it. That kind of love didn't exist for us Italians in that generation. I was engaged to Vincent and that was that. No falling in love, no romance, no passion, you will learn to love one another soon enough. Antonio's uncle agreed and sent his nephew packing as soon as he heard that there might be something between us. Poor Vincent, I hurt him deeply. He came to me one day and told me he would do his best to make me happy. Never, not even once did he condemn me. Over time I began to realize how fortunate I was to have such a sensitive person love me. He kept his promise. His warmth and love helped to mend my broken heart. As the years passed, my love for Vincent grew and he fully conquered my heart. After our first child I can say I never loved a man more than him, who was my second choice."

"Did you ever hear from Antonio?"

"Never, I thought of him from time to time but I didn't miss him. Vincent and I had a wonderful marriage and he didn't let the memory of Antonio haunt him. He never looked backwards, always ahead. He never tried to change my feeling for Antonio. He just let me fill up on his love for me. You can't change Monica's feelings for Bob. Don't try! If it is meant to be, you will have your Monica. Pasqual, you may get a chance to be understanding and like my Vincent to show a different kind of love with your sensitivity and patience. Pasqual, I am a simple woman but I know that love can be a raging sea and that same sea can be calm, tranquil, smooth and beautiful. Be a good boy, say your prayers, pray for Bob and Monica and yourself and don't give up. I have a feeling you will have a place in Monica's life." Aunt Theresa, who was not usually so wordy, leaned over and kissed a distraught and tearful Pasqual on the forehead. With that he left in silence.

Chapter Twenty-four

"How are you feeling?"

Bob lifted his head, staring at the nurse. His head felt as heavy as the first bowling ball he picked up as a kid. He couldn't see very clearly either. "My God, what has happened to me?"

"How are you feeling?"

"I can't see."

"Don't worry, it's from the anesthesia. It'll clear up soon."

"I feel weak."

"You should, you just lost a lot of blood. If you look to your right you'll see you are receiving a final pint of blood. That should do it."

"Is the operation over?"

"Yes, all over. You need rest, but first your family and friends want to see you. But they can only stay for a few minutes."

"Is Monica here? I hope grandmom is okay."

"Bob, I think everyone's here."

"Nurse, what time is it?"

"It's seven p.m." Bob turned his head as the door opened. It was his father with grandmom holding onto his arm. When Jim got close enough to Bob he bent over and kissed him on the forehead and said for only his ears to hear, "I'm taking care of grandmom. This time I won't let you down." Bob smiled and said nothing.

"Nurse, do you think my son could hear me."

"He's a little dazed, but I am sure he heard you. You have to give him time to come around."

Jim felt awkward. He had nothing to say and all grandmom could do was finger her rosaries and weep. "Grandmom, I think we should go and let Monica come in and visit. He may come in and out of sleep for another day." They left quietly and Monica and Father Maguire entered while Bob was still asleep. Monica went up to his ear and whispered, "I am here sweetheart, and so is Father Maguire."

"Monica, would you join me in the 'Our Father?"

"Of course, Father!"

As they were praying Bob opened his eyes and added his amen to theirs. Bob made an effort to speak. "Relax, honey, don't exert yourself!" Bob got agitated. He shook his head, no. "Not much time, not much time."

"Please Bob, you're going to pull out the IVs."

"Bob, I know what you are worried about. I will represent you to Mrs. Brown."

Bob calmed down at the sound of those words. His eyes were fixed on Father Maguire. "I know the sorrow that is in your heart. I remember what you told me. You had hoped to meet with Mrs. Brown and tell her how sorry you were for what has happened. Am I correct, Bob?"

"Yes, Father."

"Well, I will visit Mrs. Brown. In the newspaper they mentioned how her congregation was rallying behind her. I'll probably make the initial contact through her minister." Once again, Bob nodded. "Now, you must take this to heart. Everything is in God's hands. His will be done. Trust Him!" Monica held Bob's hand as he fell asleep.

Chapter Twenty-five

Two weeks had passed. The Pontellos and Bob's family had visited the hospital every day, if only for an update on the boy's condition. Always the same encouraging report, a slight infection but the infection should break soon. This time, however, Dr. Hand admitted to Monica and Bob's family some deep concerns that the infection might be getting worse. He was not responding really well to any anti-biotic.

Bob's dad wanted to escape through his addiction, but something held him back from throwing everything away and visiting Murphy's Bar. He wasn't there for his wife; he was determined not to make the same mistake twice.

At the bad news, Monica cried uncontrollably. She was sure that Bob was lost. Her moods were strange of late. She was hypersensitive, easily hurt, restless, and couldn't keep her food down. Everyone thought it was because of Bob and in an indirect way it was because of Bob and her. She visited Bob everyday after work.

The Pontellos were worried about their daughter. They urged her to see their family physician. Maria extracted promises from Monica that she would take care of her own health and make an appointment with the doctor herself. The bouts of vomiting were getting more frequent, almost every meal and the dry heaves in the morning.

One Sunday afternoon, when the sensitive stomach episodes had increased, the Pontellos received a telephone call from Father Maguire. "Is Monica there? This is Father Maguire."

"Hello, Father! This is her dad."

"Monica is such a fine young lady. You must be very proud of her."

"Yes, we are and we are extremely grateful to you for visiting so often and relieving Monica of so many of her burdens. My daughter has the deepest respect for you." Before

Dominic could call his daughter to the phone, she was standing beside him.

"Father, did you hear anything from Mrs. Brown? Are you sure she won't see him?" Father had only bad news. "Oh Bob will be so disappointed. What are you going to tell him?"

"The truth, of course!" Monica agreed to meet Father Maguire at the hospital that evening. Mr. Pontello would accompany his daughter. Monica had put down the receiver. Aunt Theresa said, "Monica, you look like you are in a daze." Monica just stared blankly ahead. "Monica, did you hear me? What's wrong?"

"Mrs. Brown read about Bob's version of the murder and doesn't believe a word of it. Father planned to pick her up and take her to the hospital to meet Bob. She refused. 'What good will it do my son for me to meet with his murderer. There's just nothing to say.'

"Monica, you surely can understand the poor woman's feelings. She doesn't know Bob from Adam. And as for you, young lady, it's time for you to take care of yourself. I have a strong suspicion I know what's wrong with you, but never mind. Did you make your appointment with Doctor Stein?"

"Tomorrow!"

"Some things can't wait." Maria came into the room.

"Theresa, let up. Her father will take her to the hospital, and that will make her feel better."

By the time they reached the hospial, Monica was calm. She entered the room and found Bob cranked up in sitting position. Bob slowly smiled at his Monica and she kissed him on the lips. "Father Maguire will be here soon."

"Father's become such a good friend to us, Monica."

"Do you feel better today, sweetheart?"

"I think I'm getting a little stronger. Don't worry about me. I'll be fine."

Father Maguire entered the room. "How are you today, Bob?"

"I'm feeling stronger."

"Well, I have some news from Mrs. Brown. It's not good." Bob's eyes widened, anticipating the worst. She refuses to see you. She thinks, despite your allegations, that you are her son's murderer." Bob just leaned his head deep into his pillow and filled up.

"She did not think it would serve any good purpose. She is resentful not only of you, but also of the entire gang. However, she was gracious enough to take my phone calls. She spoke with me several times, and I almost thought I had reached some understanding when she hung up on me. I think she is a very compassionate woman and going through a great struggle inside of her. She is unquestionably a religious woman and a practicing Christian. Bob, you just have to understand, she's just not ready to face her son's killer. You have to continue to pray that God will grant you your wish. You mustn't give up on prayer. God has not abandoned us. There is still hope."

Bob had not listened to the encouraging words. He sunk into a deep and quiet despair. He was beyond consolation. He had hoped for forgiveness from Floyd's mother. If she could understand, maybe God could forgive him and last of all, maybe Bob could forgive himself.

Chapter Twenty-six

After singing the sermon hymn, "Precious Lord," the pastor mounted the pulpit in a slow dignified gait. "Brothers and sisters, The Father sent his only son, Jesus, to save us from our sins, so that we may have eternal life. What a precious gift, what a generous Father." Thus began the sermon of the Pastor of the First Baptist Church of Faith, Hope and Love.

"Amen, praise the Lord," echoed throughout the congregation.

"Jesus hung on the cross beaten and bleeding and instead of crying out insults and injury, he prayed, 'Father, forgive them, for they know not what they do!'"

"Amen, alleluia," filled the sanctuary as the congregation and the preacher were actively engaged. A frail looking woman sat quietly in the rear of the Church. The words, "Father, forgive them for they know not what they do," resounded through her soul with a special and most personal meaning. Her mind drifted back to when she was eleven years old.

Everyday in the summertime Janney and her sister Thelma would bring their father his lunch. This one afternoon Thelma had a dentist's appointment and Janney went alone to bring her father his lunch. He worked as a janitor for the Municipal Court. When she arrived at the courthouse, she went immediately to the janitor's quarters. As she approached the room the door was slightly ajar, enough to hear the conversation taking place within. She peeked in and saw her daddy sitting on a chair and being interrogated by two white men, who were probably her daddy's bosses or some official deputies. She listened to the humiliating conversation between her father and these awful men. "Mr. Smith, I just could not hold my water. Sir, I worked here for more than ten years and I never disobeyed the rules."

"You know not to use the white man's rest room. You know people complain if they see a colored person in there."

"I know, I know, Sir, but I couldn't help it. Lately I have been having problems holding my water. I didn't want to have an accident in the hall."

"Okay Roger, we'll let you go this time. You've been with us a long time and have been a faithful employee, but don't let it happen again."

"No Sir, Mr. Smith, no Sir!"

"You're a good colored. Stay that way and you won't have any trouble."

"Yes, Sir, Mr. Hastings." As the deputies were leaving, Janney quickly hid behind a staircase. When they were out of sight, she ran into the room to see her daddy. He was still sitting in the chair sweating and breathing heavily.

"Janney, honey," he said, turning slightly in the chair. "What are you doing here?"

"I brought you your lunch. How could you let those men treat you that way?"

"Don't worry yourself, honey."

"Some day, Daddy, I'll get even with them."

"No, honey, I don't want you to talk that way."

"Daddy, after what they did to you, I'll always hate white people."

"Janney, don't you realize if you hate someone, that hate controls you? It's not right how our people are treated. But we cannot plan revenge. Our heavenly father sees all. Love, Janney, and love alone will conquer our enemies. The enemy is prejudice, fear and misunderstanding. Jesus died for all. Look what they did to him. They crucified him, yet he forgave them. He is our model. He will make all things right. Don't let anger destroy the love within you." When she recalled what her father had said about Jesus it resonated with the minister's preaching and brought her out of her reminiscences.

The minister was near concluding his sermon. "Brothers and Sisters, let us examine our consciences on this beautiful Sunday morning. Let us ask ourselves, is there someone we know that needs our forgiveness?" By now Janney was touched even more deeply by the sermon. The pastor said, "And remember what Jesus said. If you have an argument to settle with your brother, first settle with him and then return to the altar to make your sacrifice. The Lord wants a sacrifice of a clean and forgiving heart. Say Amen Somebody!"

"Amen, Pastor, Amen," resounded through the church.

"The Lord bless all you good Christian people. Our service will conclude with the singing of "The Old Rugged Cross." After the service don't forget that all are invited downstairs to the social hall, where the Lady's auxiliary will be serving coffee and cake."

Janney was clearly torn and moved by the service: her father, her poor Floyd and that white boy wanting to talk to her. She rolled the handkerchief around her index finger and repeated, I can't forgive that boy for killing my son, and several old friends and sympathetic parishioners offered her renewed consolation on their way to the reception downstairs. Pastor Crawford joined the group and asked if the ladies wouldn't mind excusing Janney and himself because they had something important to discuss. The pastor knew his congregation, and was especially conscious of this one parishioner"s unique cross. He said, "Janney, come into my study. I think your heart is heavily burdened."

"Pastor, I am overwhelmed by grief and your sermon on forgiveness has further confused me. I am having a difficult time overcoming my feelings of anger and revenge against my son's murderer. You know he wants to talk to me."

"Janney you are a model Christian."

"Oh, no I'm not. I'm filled with anger and hatred, hardly the feelings of a good Christian."

"Janney, you know the Lord worked on will, not feeling alone. He didn't want to be crucified. It was the only way to show his love. I don't want to sell you on any course of action. What you do must bring you peace of mind and heart, not confusion and despair. As you know Father Maguire called me."

"Pastor, I know, he is a good man."

"He has no intention of causing you pain."

"I understand that he is a man of the cloth. It's his job to help people. I don't blame him."

"What Father Maguire asked you to do is difficult. No one would blame you if you said, flat out, no! But Janney, maybe you need to visit the boy to find out what really happened."

"What are you saying?"

"There are circumstances that Father Maguire revealed to me, which might give you peace. There is also a possibility that there may be two victims murdered."

"Pastor, I just can't handle any more pain. I'm not like my father. He was strong, but I can't forgive. That boy and his friends killed my Floyd for no good reason, just because he was colored." The pastor gave up. She wasn't ready to understand that Bob himself took a bullet, which might be fatal and was under the gun to retrieve the knife. He just hugged and patted Janney's back as she cried uncontrollably for her disturbed conscience, her son and her daddy. In this state of agitation and confusion she addressed a prayer to Floyd. "How am I going to live without you? Jesus take care of my boy and have pity on me."

Chapter Twenty-seven

The next day Monica called Dr. Stein's office to set up an appointment. He would be able to see her at three o'clock. Mrs. Pontello, relieved that her daughter had taken the initiative, wanted to accompany her. Monica wouldn't hear of it. "Mom, please stay and help out. I'll be fine. After the doctor's visit I want to head over to the hospital to visit Bob. It's a lovely day. I think I'll walk over to Dr. Stein's and take the trolley to the hospital."

"Monica, your father wants me to go with you. I'm sure he and Aunt Theresa can handle the store just fine."

"Please Mom, let me go by myself. I'm a grown up now. Besides I feel great today."

"Have it your way, but just promise you'll be home for dinner. I don't want to argue with the sick."

"I promise I'll be home for supper." As Monica walked up Ninth Street, over to Eleventh and Catherine, she passed several tidy, well-kept row homes. The Halloween decorations in the front windows reminded her of her own happy childhood. Her mother would take infinite care to make her the most original costume. When Halloween night arrived, no matter how many times her mother had fitted her for her outfit, she was always surprised at how intricate and cleverly put together the costume was. It was just like Christmas. She remembered going out with friends, with her father lurking in the background making sure nothing went wrong. She never felt more secure.

In later years she continued the practice of dressing up for Halloween, and she would greet the children at the door in costume. It was only just a year ago when she and Pasqual dressed up as Raggedy Ann and Raggedy Andy. They couldn't stop laughing when they laid eyes on one another. Pasqual said, 'Monica, we'll make this a family custom. When the children arrive, it will only intensify our joy." How far they had come from that night? She was not without pity for her fiancé whom

106

she imagined must be in great pain over the situation with Bob. How life changes! She was having such a nice reminiscence with herself; she arrived at the office before she realized. She opened the door to the red brick row home with a discrete sign hanging from it's own metal stand next to the marble steps. Monica greeted the nurse, "Hello, Mrs. Smith."

"Oh hello, Monica. The last patient left a little early, and Dr. Stein will see you immediately. Just go right in."

Monica entered the inner sanctum to an immaculately clean room with the doctor's desk, roll and sway back chair, and an examining table covered with a clean sheet. These were the days when plastic was not in common use. Monica said, "Dr. Stein, thank you for seeing me on such short notice."

"Never too busy to see the little girl I brought into the world. How are you Monica?"

"Oh, Doctor, I don't know what I am going to do." Monica surprised herself and broke into tears.

"Monica, sit down. Make yourself comfortable! I've read the papers. I know all about what happened to your family."

"As if that wasn't enough, I am not feeling well. I am moody. I can't hold down my meals, especially in the morning when I wake up nauseous."

"How long have you had these symptoms?"

"A little over two weeks."

"Monica, if I didn't know better, I would say it sounds like you're pregnant. Now you must be honest with me. I am your physician. Have you had sexual relations with your boyfriend? It won't do not to answer truthfully. And please no embarrassment."

"Dr. Stein, we had relations, but just once."

"Well, I won't know until I examine you, but I strongly suspect you are pregnant. If it's the right time, one time is enough."

"Oh God, what am I going to do?"

"You must tell the father. Do you think he will take responsibility for the child?"

"I don't know if he can."

"What do you mean?"

"Bob O'Connor is the father."

"Oh I see, the boy in the hospital. Well he still has to be told. And, of course, you must confide in your parents. They won't let you down. Let me examine you. Get on the examining table, and put your feet in the stirrups."

She left the office after forcing a cordial farewell for Mrs. Smith. Her eyes were red and her complexion was pale. As she waited at the trolley stop she prayed God would please make him well, "For the three of us, Lord." She spoke audibly but under her breath.

She arrived at the hospital in what seemed a very short time. When she entered the room, Bob was asleep. She shook him gently and woke him. "Bob, you must listen to me. I have something very important to share with you." She hesitated a long while, waiting for him to become fully conscious, "You're going to be a father." He slowly pulled himself together and she repeated herself. "You're going to be a father." Slowly moving himself into sitting position he said, "A father?"

Monica smiled, and nodded a yes. He gradually smiled broadly. "I can't believe it, you're pregnant?"

"Bob, it's true, I'm pregnant."

"I am going to be a father." Finally some good news for somber times! Then Bob sunk into a deep sleep.

Chapter Twenty-eight

Bob awoke again and lay there staring at the ceiling. His head was sunk deep into the pillow. Monica leaned over and kissed him. Bob's body twitched. "I'm sorry, darling. I didn't mean to startle you." She wasn't sure he had heard her when she told him she was pregnant. She had no desire of going through it all over again but thought she must. Before she could open her mouth Bob said, "Monica, we're going to have a baby. Real proof that we love one another! You know, I still feel bad about Mrs. Brown not wanting to see me, but this news gives me some hope that God has not abandoned us. Have you told your parent yet?"

"No, not yet, Bob. I don't have the courage. I am going to tell them tonight at supper. I would have rather told them with you at my side, but that is out of our hands."

"I just wish I weren't so sick."

"You'll get better, Bob. Don't lose faith."

"Yeah, now I have good reasons to get better, you and the baby."

"And Mrs. Brown may come around yet. Stranger things have happened. Father Maguire thinks so."

"And when I come home, we'll get married and I'll be the best damned husband and father on Ninth Street. Oh, who am I kidding? I ain't getting better. I'm gonna die and leave you and the baby alone. Thank God for your parents and Pasqual."

"Oh Bob, please don't talk that way." And they both started to cry. Bob broke away from their embrace and said, "Monica, I am really happy about the baby, but I am so sorry I got you into this situation."

"Bob, it's just as much my fault as yours. You didn't force me to make love to you. I wanted to. I love you with all my heart."

"Monica, don't forget the courts. I could end up in jail for involuntary manslaughter. I don't think any jury would believe me, and I might have to go away for a while."

"You know my parents will help until you can take over your duties as husband and father." When the nurse came into the room Bob shouted out that he was going to be a father. For the first time in his recovery, Monica truly believed that he would get better. She felt in her soul that this baby was the blessing that would accomplish the miracle she had been praying for. Then he said, "Nurse, I'm mighty hungry. I hope you have a tray for me. I could eat a horse."

"Bob, I'm going home to tell my parents and eat a horse myself. I'm tired of crying and being sad. The doctor gave me some pills to stop the nausea. I'm going to put on a glad face. And think positive." They kissed like they were married and Monica went home.

Monica went to open the front door, but realized she hadn't brought her keys with her when she left the house earlier in the day. She rang the doorbell and Mrs. Simone, a neighbor called over to her. She was nicknamed the "Sentinel" of Wharton Street. Her home was directly opposite the Pontellos' and the streets weren't wide in this part of South Philadelphia. Nothing got past her notice. "Monica, how is that boy who got shot in your store, who used to work for you?"

"He's coming along fine, Mrs. Simone."

"How long have you known him?" Monica rolled her eyes praying for someone to open the door. Suddenly, Aunt Theresa's welcomed face came to the door. She yelled across the street in Italian, "Hello and Good Night Mrs. Simone, we're having supper. Go watch the evening news, catch up on world events." With that the door opened and slammed shut almost in one smooth move. "I got no time for that busybody."

"Thank God you answered the door."

"What did you do, forget your keys? I thought so. What did the doctor say?"

"Aunt Theresa, not here." Theresa leaned over and whispered in Monica's ear, "You're pregnant aren't you? Let's get out of the vestibule. I'll be praying when you tell your father."

Father and mother accosted Monica, and she asked everyone to sit around the supper table. Mrs. Pontello blurted, "Well, what did the doctor say?"

"I'm fine."

"So why were you so sick?"

"I'm in good health."

"So why the doctor visit?"

"Mom and Dad, Aunt Theresa… Aunt Theresa, please, tell them."

"She's pregnant. You're going to have a grandchild. Let's have a few smiles. It happens all the time to families in Italy. You thought it would be different here. And if he ever gets better he'll marry her."

"Oh, Aunt Theresa, don't talk so negative. Of course, he'll get better."

Mr. Pontello remained speechless for sometime. Monica knew he was hurting. She kneeled down in front of him, "Pop, I love you. Don't let this baby that makes Bob and me so happy, make you sad. Be happy for us. It's a new life. God wanted it and let it happen. Think about how you wanted to be a grandparent. Please, don't close your heart to me. This is Monica. I love you."

"Monica honey, I am sad for you. This isn't the way it should have happened."

"Daddy, I need you. I can't make it without your help and love. Mom, Dad, I need you."

Mr. Pontello said, "My little girl, my dear sweat little girl is going to be a mother. Maria our baby needs us." Maria and Theresa looked on as father and daughter cried on each other's shoulders.

Chapter Twenty-nine

Shortly after Bob received the news of Monica's pregnancy, the thought of becoming a father seemed to have sparked a recovery in him. His appetite returned. His temperature fell, and he even felt well enough to receive a visit from a court appointed attorney. He began preparing for his trial. In three days, just as fast as he rallied, he returned to his feverish state and lost appetite.

Dr. Hand entered the room and noticed his untouched lunch tray lying off to the side. "What's the matter, Bob? No appetite today? Let me take your temperature." While waiting for the thermometer to do its work Bob thought of Monica and the baby. He knew the Pontellos would take care of them, but he wanted more for Monica. He wanted her to have a life, not the drudgery of single parenting and the social stigma of having a child out of wedlock. She deserved better and his baby needed a father, not like himself, raised with an absentee dad.

"Bob, your temperature is elevated."

"What is it, Doc?"

"It's one hundred and two. But don't be overly concerned, we've been there before."

"You know, Doc, I'm going to become a father."

"I heard all about it. Congratulations, Mazel Tov!"

"Do you think I'll be around in June when the baby arrives?"

"Don't be so pessimistic. You have to live in hope. I certainly hope we find the correct anti-biotic. I think you should only allow yourself optimistic thoughts, anything else will not help you improve your condition."

"Doc, please be honest with me. I heard the nurse read my chart and she was talking to herself about a very high number. Can't you tell me what she said."

"Bob, I don't believe in lying to patients. She saw that your white blood cell count was twenty-five thousand. But I've seen them come down rapidly. As fast as they rise they often fall. I've even seen higher ones. Your body's ability to fight can improve. Your white blood cell can go even higher and you could still make it to a full recovery."

"Are you telling me there is hope?"

"Most definitely! But I wouldn't go throwing high numbers around your family. It would only upset them unnecessarily. The situation is distressing but not any reason to expect the worst. Everyday you keep fighting your chances of staying alive increase. Any information you give your family won't change anything." Bob looked at him long and hard to try and discern whether or not he could believe him, something he wanted to do in the worst way. He decided to believe Dr. Hand, who had never given him pause to doubt either his medical expertise or his sincerity.

"Thanks Doc, and I haven't mentioned to you how grateful I was that you arranged to have the police guard removed from outside my door. It has made it so much easier on my family and Monica's."

"Bob, you're welcome. Now I think you should at least eat one thing on your tray and get some rest. If I can do anything for you, just tell the nurse to send for me." With those final instructions Dr. Hand, a tall gentleman with graying temples and a thin body, left the room wearing his white lab coat where his name was embroidered on the upper left pocket. He left with dignity and grace. These were the times when physicians were held in high esteem, at or above the level of clergymen.

The phone rang as soon as Dr. Hand closed the door.

"Hello, this is the front desk. I wish to speak with Bob O'Connor."

"I'm Bob O'Connor!"

"We have a Mrs. Brown here at the desk. She says that you wanted to see her, and she is not on our visitors' list. Shall we send her up?" Bob was speechless and mystified. He never expected to see Mrs. Brown. "Hello, is this Bob O'Connor?"

"Yes, of course, please send her up, and thank you very much." She came and what'll I say? Oh God help me. His pulse raced.

Mrs. Brown was in the elevator, on her way. *What do I say to the man who killed my child? What did Pastor Crawford mean when he said I might have to visit the boy to find out what really happened? Do I need to know more? I know who killed my boy.* She reached the tenth floor. As the door opened she said aloud, "God, help me!" As she stepped out of the elevator she read Bob's room number 1020. I don't have to go in there. Why am I torturing myself? I should just get on the elevator and leave. Then she saw her daddy's face, his soft gentle eyes, his lifetime of good example, a model of self-restraint and triumph over prejudice. The picture and memory of her loving father pushed her along where she would not go. *Okay Dad, this one's for you, stay with me.* A dark skinned woman appeared in the doorway. Bob turned and their eyes met.

Chapter Thirty

"Mrs. Brown, please come in!" Nodding her head she greeted him with a pleasant good afternoon. "Well, you wanted to see me. Here I am. What do you want from me?" Bob said nothing. "Please tell me, what you expect from me?"

Bob lowered his head and said, "I know what I did was wrong and that I have done you a terrible injustice. And that saying I am sorry, and I am very sorry, just isn't enough."

"I'm listening."

"I did not intend to kill Floyd. It was an accident and the result of external force."

"Accident? He was stabbed through the heart with your prints on the knife. The police suggested it was a racially motivated influence. Is that what you meant by external force?"

"No, no, no they got it wrong."

"There were two witnesses. Now, how can you tell me it was an accident?"

"I can see it will be difficult to convince you otherwise, but I have to try. I feel I am running out of time."

"I'm still listening. I haven't gone away. You want to convince me so that you can ease your conscience."

"Mrs. Brown, my conscience will never be eased, but I do need forgiveness and to let you know what happened that night." Mrs. Brown moved slowly toward the chair next to the bed. "It's clear to me you had a lot of anger in your heart for my son and his friends."

"No Mrs. Brown, my mother didn't raise me that way. She was a good Christian woman like yourself, who raised me proper; not to hate colored people. She taught me we were all God's children." Mrs. Brown fought to hold back the tears, wanting to believe that people existed, white folk, who weren't bigoted and full of hatred because of the color of a person's skin. She wanted to cry for the whole world, for all black people who suffered indignities and for all those who chose to forgive. How easy hatred would have been! She said, "You and your friends tried to chase him away from the carnival. Why? Because they were Negroes, now isn't that hatred?"

"Yes it is, and I'm no better than my friends. I went along with them, because I didn't want them to reject me. My mom had just been buried the day before, and I was trying to forget."

"Sonny, you know better than that. You can't never forget the death of a parent, and the more you run from pain the more it dogs you."

"I know now and I learned the hard way, but I want you to know how it happened. Please be patient a little more."

"I ain't going nowhere."

"We were all drinking that night. John, the gang leader, spotted Floyd and his friends. He wanted to chase them from the carnival back to their own neighborhood. One of my gang pulled a knife on Floyd, and tried to stick him. Floyd took the knife from him. In the struggle the gang member was cut. John was angry, and told me to get the knife from Floyd. Floyd was panicked and afraid to hand over the knife. I told John we should leave. He called me a coward. He put his gun to my head, and said he would blow me away if I didn't get the knife from Floyd. I had no choice. All I wanted to do was get the knife from Floyd. We struggled. At one point we both had our hands on the knife. Floyd was on top of me. At that very moment John kicked Floyd in the back. Floyd fell on me and the knife and that is how I became a murderer." Mrs. Brown by this time had taken refuge in a chair and was crying holding her head up with one arm leaning on the bed. It was more than she could suffer having the murder of her son so vividly depicted. Every word, every action had the ring of truth. "Please believe me Mrs. Brown, I didn't want to kill your son, honest, I didn't want to kill him."

Mrs.Brown looked up with her tear stained face and saw that Bob was only a boy himself, the same age as her son, and if she could trust the newspaper accounts, he was facing death himself. Her soul grew like a powerful wind fed by yet another wind feeding upon their own momentum. Her spirit was like a breeze that turns leaves into whirlpools and sways trees under a shining sun over a clear blue sky.

"Bob, hate and anger will not bring Floyd back. I don't wish you dead." Reaching for his hand she said, "I believe that you did not intend to kill my son. I forgive you. May God help me and you too." Bob cried and kissed the offered hand. Father Maguire entered the room. He stopped suddenly. "Mrs. Brown!" She nodded and gently pulled her hand away. Without a word she quietly left the room.

Chapter Thirty-one

Father Maguire accompanied Mrs. Brown to the elevator and decided to wait until the Pontellos visited sometime between five and six. When he looked at his watch he knew it wouldn't be that long of a wait. He intended to spend the time just sitting quietly with Bob and praying his rosary if Bob was asleep. He entered the room and said, "Mrs. Brown is certainly a good person. I am so happy she came." Bob did not respond. Father noticed his eyes were open and staring at the ceiling. "Bob, did you hear me?" Again there was no response. Father tapped him on the shoulder, "Bob, can I get you something? Is something wrong?" There was no answer. Instinctively Father Maguire blessed himself and Bob, "God have mercy on your soul." He called for the nurse who checked his vital signs. They sent for Dr. Hand. Beyond a doubt Bob was dead. Father received permission to administer Extreme Unction. Dr. Hand, though not a Christian himself, waited reverently for the end of the sacrament with his head bowed. "Father Maguire, it is so difficult to lose a patient so young and in the full bloom of youth. I wish there was some oil in your case that could heal me of this pain."

"There is, Dr. Hand! As it says in your scriptures, 'I am the Lord of life and death.' You and I wait upon the Lord, and it isn't proper for us servants to question God's will. You have done your job. I am witness to that. You have executed your duties well and to the fullest extent of your powers and gifts. Be at peace, brother." With that father bowed his head and prayed Kaddish. As soon as he began Dr. Hand joined him. In those days many priests often learned Jewish prayers as they learned their biblical Hebrew. That day it brought peace and blessing to a good physician.

Father sat with Bob the minutes before the arrival of the Pontellos. When they entered the room Monica knew instinctively by the look on Father Maguire's face that Bob was dead. Monica felt only loss. She threw herself on her lover almost as if she had flown through the air. She showered him with kisses and tears like Mary Magdalene at the foot of Jesus. She wouldn't get up. She started dragging Bob's arm up as if trying to wake a drunken spouse. Then she tried two arms and Bob fell back, lifeless. A more dramatic panic would come later when she realized her child had no father and she would have no husband. The shame she had brought to her family name would only muddle things worse.

"Monica," Maria called her name in vain. She only stopped when she heard a familiar voice say, "Monica, Monica!" He spoke with gentleness and authority, and it sounded strangely out of place. She let go of Bob's arms and slowly turned to see Pasqual. "What are you doing here?"

"I thought you might need me."

"Pasqual, I don't know what I am going to do."

He tenderly drew her away from the corpse. She yielded to his masculine arm around her shoulder. He said, "I understand your loss. I came to help. Everything will be all right. I promise." With that the family left with Father Maguire and began the mourning process.

Chapter Thirty-two

Bob's family could not afford to give him a proper burial. Jim O'Connor's recent change of lifestyle left little time for the accumulation of money. The Pontellos needed no request. They offered to bury Bob as a member of their family and enter him in the family plot. Father Maguire and Dominic planned the funeral. The Requiem Mass was celebrated at St. Nicholas, where Bob first met Father Maguire. The somber black vestments captured the pain of his death and burial. Bob was laid to rest at Holy Cross Cemetery. The only relief from the suffering and tears came at the traditional meal served at the Pontellos. At the meal, which was more like a banquet, every Italian specialty was served: Genoa salami, cappacola, provolone, penne rigati in red sauce, meatballs and sausage, hard rolls, Sarcone's bread and pastries by Termines. There was something deep down in human beings that want to celebrate at the most serious and debilitating times, the hope of resurrection and the endurance of love through death. This was not a funeral banquet; it was a celebration of hope.

There was even a place for reconciliation and forgiveness. The last to stay were Bob's grandmother and his father. Mr. Pontello extended his hand in friendship when he and grandmom were leaving. "Jim, if you want, there is always a job for you at Pontellos."

"Dominic, I appreciate your offer, but I already called my old paper hanging job, and they agreed to give me another chance. I can't thank you enough for all you've done for my family, and I am ashamed of all the times I harassed you when I was drunk, and all the run ins I had with Aunt Theresa. I have already asked her forgiveness, and now it's time to ask yours."

"Jim, we are family. We have the same grandchild and everything else was in the past. Think nothing of it. There is always room for you and yours at our table. We'll see a lot of one another once the baby is born." For the first time that day grandmom's face lit up. Dominic said, "Mrs. McDermott, you'll be a great grandmother." When Bob's family left, a quiet fell over the house. Theresa said, "Maria and Dominic, go to bed. It's late. Monica can help; she won't go to bed for a long time. There's no reason why we should all miss a good night's rest."

"Theresa, I couldn't take advantage of you like that."

"Come on, Maria. We're sisters. I'll sleep overnight. Even though I'm older than you are, I am stronger. Being a widow is good for your upper arm strength, and the broom is my specialty." Dominic and Maria were so drained it wasn't difficult to listen to Theresa. But Theresa had an ulterior motive for her apparent generosity.

"Monica, if you need me, just…"

"I know, Mom, I know. Don't worry. I can't go to bed just yet."

Monica and Aunt Theresa were wrapping up the left over meats, desserts and hot foods that would spoil if left out. The doorbell rang. "Who could that be at this late hour?"

"Maybe one of the neighbors."

"Probably that busy body, Mrs. Simone. I'll get it, Monica." When she opened the door she broke into a broad smile. "Pasqual, I'm glad you came."

"Theresa, I know it's late, but I had to talk to Monica."

"That's okay. Monica is in the kitchen. Monica will be glad to see you. She doesn't know it just yet, but she really needs you."

"Theresa, it's more like I need her." Theresa directed Pasqual to the kitchen but she remained in the parlor. When Monica recognized her surprise visitor, she brightened despite her grief. Pasqual gave Monica a kiss on the cheat. Monica said, "I saw you at church, and I wondered why you didn't come for the meal. Sit down. Let me get you something to eat."

"Monica, I am too upset to eat. I went to the Mass to pray for you, Bob and the baby. I watched you at the service and your expression and your tears projected the love and the pain you were feeling. It was as if a part of you died. It was as if you were united in spirit. It all expressed a love that I know I had never felt. I guess you could call it true love."

"Pasqual, I've never heard you talk this way."

"I surprised myself. It was the love you had for one another that helped me see so clearly. It helped me realize the deep and passionate love I have for you. I always knew I loved you, but I never realized until now the depths of my love for you."

"So you do understand the love Bob and I had."

"Yes I do, and it has given me the courage to ask a favor of you. Would you allow me to take care of you and the baby?"

"How could that be, Pasqual? We don't have that kind of love?"

"Monica, there are many kinds of love and what I feel for you falls under the category of love."

"It can't be, it shouldn't be. You deserve better. I am an unwed mother and a widow without being married."

"Monica, just listen, please. You have a baby to take care of. The baby needs a father. I want to be its father, just like adoption. I can't think of any better person to adopt than a child of someone I love. I would love the baby as my own. You should have a husband. You know how mean our people can be to unwed mothers. We can make a life for each other. You wouldn't be a woman shamed and your baby wouldn't be a bastard and it would all happen with someone who loves you intensely, who expects nothing but the opportunity to live with you as brother and sister."

"Now that would really be unfair. I would be getting much more than I could ever hope of giving. I don't know if I could ever have sexual relations with anyone. I don't know if I will ever be able to again."

"Monica, without any pressure at all, I am willing to wait for you, as long as it takes, and if it never happens, at least I am with the only person I have ever loved in my entire life in this whole wide world. I want to marry you out of love. I want to take care of you out of devotion; the love I have for you would not let me do anything less."

"I don't know Pasqual. I am scared and confused."

"I promise you I will never try to take his place, never try to erase his memory." Reaching for Monica's hand he said, "I want to marry you." She gently placed her hand on his. "Monica, I want to marry you. All I ask is that you think about it."

Chapter Thirty-three

Monica sat on the sofa pondering her recent encounter with an intense and generous Pasqual. Aunt Theresa entered holding a tray with two cups of tea and some biscotti.

"Monica, I thought you could use a cup of tea."

"Thank you, Aunt Theresa! Do you know what Pasqual just did? He proposed to me. He offered to help me solve all my problems."

"Do I know? That boy is in love with you. You are a lucky woman. He won't let go without a struggle. Just think, as young as you are, you've had two wonderful men in your life. My God, you're following in my footsteps."

They both laughed. "Seriously Monica, what are you going to do?"

"I don't know. It would be so easy for me to accept Pasqual's proposal. The baby would have a father, and I would spare the family shame."

"True, you'd have a husband, a good man who truly loves you."

"But I can't love him like Bob."

"From what I could hear, he didn't ask you to. From what I accidentally heard he is willing to marry you, and he understands the situation." Monica smiled at Aunt Theresa's benevolent interference.

"Aunt Theresa, it isn't fair to him. I couldn't have sex with him or anybody. I need time to heal."

"Do I have to tell you what he said about sex?"

"No, he said he would wait, even a lifetime."

"Exactly! And who are you to tell people what's fair or unfair to them. Monica? Life isn't fair, never was, never will be. Monica, Bob's dead and he's not coming back and you have the Mrs..Simones waiting to tear down your reputation, and a neighborhood full of the next generation of boys and girls who will call your son a bastard and you a whore. And you have a man who is willing to share the gift of his love and life with you. In time you may grow to love Pasqual more deeply."

"That's what he said. Have you been coaching him?"

"Maybe! But remember, any love you show him cannot take away any of the love you have for Bob. Now drink your tea, go to bed and get some sleep. This story can have a happy ending. Just open your heart up a little wider and start thinking of yourself with all the love and intensity you poured on Bob." Monica stood up and embraced Aunt Theresa and cried softly on her shoulders. "Aunt Theresa, I love you. Pray for me. Everything has happened so fast. I am scared."

Aunt Theresa pulled away and with her thumb traced the sign of the cross on Monica's forehead. "God bless you, Monica. I won't stop praying for you until you are happy again. I love you too."

Monica went to bed and Aunt Theresa sat on the sofa and pulled out her worn rosary beads and prayed the sorrowful mysteries and not without many tears for all the suffering in life, even in the lives of the young.

Chapter Thirty-four

In the rectory of St. Nicholas Church, Father Maguire declared Pasqual Greco and Monica Pontello man and wife. She wore a beige dress with a hat with an attached veil. Pasqual wore a pin striped suit with a red tie and a small knot. The Greco's, Pontellos and O'Connors were all represented. Everything was cheerful and uncomplicated. This marriage had to be lived one day at a time to reassure Monica she had made the correct decision and to test Pasqual and his generous promises. Aunt Theresa stood on the rim of the room and took it all in like some magnificent wedding cake she had made and decorated. She knew all's well that ends well and was the only one present who allowed herself the luxury of throwing rice on the emerging couple. On the rectory steps both Monica and Pasqual hugged her like she was a teddy bear. Maria and Dominic were a little baffled at the affection, but said nothing. They went to Atlantic City, the Rose Room and the shows at Steel Peer. They took pleasure in short walks on the boardwalk and the beauty of the boundless ocean: blue, green, peaceful, stormy, surging then relenting, full of mystery and eternal.

Chapter Thirty-five

Monica was stocking the kitchen cabinets with utensils while Pasqual hung a picture of the Last Supper on the wall opposite the dining room table. As he gave the nail the final blow, the doorbell rang. A round heavyset, red-faced man was at the door. "Greco residence?"

"Yes, the Greco residence."

"Sir, your bed from Sears is here."

"We've been expecting you." The large man carried in the headboard while two more slender men brought in the rest in two shifts. They set up the bed and left. Washing up before supper, Pasqual thought, what a bad way to start a new life with a new bride. It was true he didn't have to sleep on the couch anymore, but now that Monica's new bed had arrived, he could have the guestroom all to himself. He was heavily burdened sleeping in separate bedrooms.

The thought of this beautiful apartment on 8th and Catherine Streets, a block from 9th Street Market and the famous Palumbo's Night Club, a beautiful, young bride, and separate bedrooms became unbearable. After super they sat in the living room, Monica reading a novel and he just staring into space almost praying Monica would say, Pasqual come into my bed tonight and sleep with me. I want to really be your wife. He looked over at Monica who was wearing a blue sleeveless nightgown. Her legs were stunning. The thought of rubbing his hands up and down her legs made him nauseous inside. "Monica, I'm going to bed." She thought it strange of Pasqual, leaving first. He usually went to bed late. And he didn't kiss her goodnight, which was their customary practice.

Pasqual was unable to sleep. He lay there thinking, I should go straight to her room right now and tell her I love her and that I want to claim my marital rights. Enough of this brooding, Monica, you must go on with your life. I need you.

He got up out of bed and reached her door, about to turn the handle. He thought with deep regret because he didn't want things to be this way anymore, I made a promise. She needs time and I must give it to her. Like a prisoner he dragged himself slowly back to his empty bed, in the guestroom.

Chapter Thirty-six

Robert, their newborn, was sound asleep when they arrived at their apartment. Pasqual held the bassinet while Monica unlocked the door and switched on the lights. When they entered the apartment Monica took over the child. Pasqual leaned over and kissed the child. "I'll get him ready for bed and then I guess I'll turn in." Pasqual kissed her good night.

"Monica, the christening was beautiful. All the food your family and Aunt Theresa made. I'm sure everyone had a good time."

"You're right. It was a wonderful baptism. We had a long day. I'll see you in the morning." She kissed him goodnight and settled the six-week-old baby in his crib. Monica brooded over the baby's father Robert O'Connor as she leaned over the crib. Little Robert had curly hair like his father and those sky blue eyes.

She lay in bed unable to fall asleep. She kept thinking of Pasqual. She loved him for his loyalty, affection and compassion. She knew she loved him, not the same way she loved Bob, but nevertheless, real love. Now she knew what the old people meant when they said you couldn't compare apples with oranges. She even imagined what it would be like to be wrapped in Pasqual's arms. Desire ran through her body. Monica decided to go into the living room to walk off these thoughts. To her surprise Pasqual was reading the newspaper when she entered the room. He was wearing pajama bottoms and she could see his chest made manly by lifting and hard work and his long and masculine neck. "I thought you were going to bed."

"I can't sleep, Monica."

"Me neither. Should I make you some herbal tea?" They looked into one another's eyes and each could clearly read the longing in the other's gaze. Pasqual embraced her, held her tightly within his arms and kissing her passionately. "I love you, Monica."

"I love you, Pasqual. Be my husband!" He scooped her up in his arms and like a man carrying his wife over the threshold, he carried her to their common bed, and they loved one another as man and wife.

Epilogue

Five Years Later

The produce business continued to grow, but a cornerstone of the operation, Aunt Theresa, died. Aunt Theresa was sitting at her familiar spot on a stool by the shelves of fruits and vegetables. Pasqual came up to her from behind with some lunch. He leaned over and said to her, "Aunt Theresa, what are you doing sleeping on the job? And in the middle of the day!" Her eyes were shut and her head lowered. He tapped her more vigorously on the shoulder. When she didn't respond to his prodding, he realized she was gone. "Aunt Theresa, how will we ever manage without you? There will never be another like you."

She was buried in the family plot next to her husband on May 10, 1959. With Aunt Theresa gone both the Pontellos and the Grecos decided to retire and pass the business on to Pasqual and Monica. Pasqual turned into quite an entrepreneur. He decided to expand the produce store and move the meat store next to the expanded produce store. He hired four new butchers and several workers for the produce stand, now doubled in size. He managed both operations directly. He had both business and people sense. He never lost an employee unnecessarily or because of discomfort on the job. He knew how to handle people with a firm and guiding hand and he was very generous with his workers.

Monica kept the books but spent most of her time being a wife and mother. Monica did not forget Bob or his family. She often visited Mrs. McDermott even after her institutionalization for senility. Mr. O'Connor enjoyed his grandchild until he died at St. Agnes Hospital with cirrhosis of the liver at the age of fifty-eight.

It was a cold Sunday afternoon. The wind was sharp and raw, chilling to the bone. The black Chevy Cavalier pulled into the front gate of Holy Cross Cemetery. It stopped next to the

131

Pontello's family burial site. Pasqual got out first and carried a Christmas blanket of red carnations. He placed it over the grave and paused to say his prayers. Monica and the children sat in the back seat of the car. She turned to her son Bobby and handed him a rose. "Robert, hold onto this for Mommy." He had Bob's beautiful blue eyes and Monica's black hair, but only curly like his father's. Robert was anxious to get out of the car and be with his Daddy, Pasqual. Little Maria was standing on the seat of the car, precariously close to the edge. "Maria, sit down before you fall and hurt yourself. After fixing Maria's coat and hat, making sure she was dressed for the weather, she placed a rose on the front seat of the car and she and her two children went to join Pasqual.

Pasqual, who had just finished his prayers, picked up his daughter, Maria, and held her in his arms. Robert was obviously anxious to place the rose his mother had given him on the grave, as he had done countless times before. As many times as Monica had visited Bob's gravesite it had never become routine. This time was no different. She paused to look at the six foot brown marble headstone, with each family members name carved into the stone. There beneath grandfather's name was Bob O'Connor, 1936-1956. "Now, Robert!" Robert placed the rose near the headstone and bowed his head in a child's prayer like his mother and Daddy had done. With his one free hand Pasqual put his arm firmly at Monica's waist and guided her to the warm automobile.

Pasqual entered last. As soon as he was about to start the car Monica interrupted him. With the rose in her hand, which she had left on the front seat she said, "Pasqual, with all my heart and soul, I love you. I can never pay you back for your loyalty, tenderness and loving care. You are my husband till death do us part." She then leaned over and kissed him gently on his lips. Pasqual was immobilized. Tears streamed down his cheeks. It was the consummation of a new kind of love built upon suffering and patience and a sanctification of their five-year sexual bond.

About the Author

Joseph F. Ruggiero was born and raised in South Philadelphia He has spent his life working as a psychotherapist. He is an avid reader, walker, and family man. A member of the Secular Franciscan order, he leads a quiet life with his wife and family. He has founded a most successful drug and alcohol treatment facility where he has worked for the past 34 years. Even though he earns his living as a therapist, he believes deeply in the healing power of fiction: to uplift, inspire, entertain the soul, and bring about a change of values.

Made in the USA
Lexington, KY
17 November 2012